The SAPPHIRE Heist

ALSO BY LAUREN BLAKELY

The Caught Up in Love Series

(Each book in this series follows a different couple, so each book can be read separately or enjoyed as a series, since characters cross over.)
Caught Up in Her (a short prequel novella to Caught Up in Us)
Caught Up in Us
Pretending He's Mine
Trophy Husband
Stars in Their Eyes

Stand-Alone Novels

Big Rock
Mister Org@sm
Far Too Tempting
21 Stolen Kisses
Playing with Her Heart (a stand-alone Seductive Nights spin-off novel about Jill and Davis)

The No Regrets Series

The Thrill of It
The Start of Us
Every Second with You

The Seductive Nights Series

Night after Night (Julia and Clay, book one)
After This Night (Julia and Clay, book two)

One More Night (Julia and Clay, book three)
Nights with Him (a stand-alone novel about Michelle and Jack)
Forbidden Nights (a stand-alone novel about Nate and Casey)

The Sinful Nights Series

Sweet Sinful Nights
Sinful Desire
Sinful Longing
Sinful Love

The Fighting Fire Series

Burn for Me (Smith and Jamie)
Melt for Him (Megan and Becker)
Consumed by You (Travis and Cara)

The SAPPHIRE Heist

LAUREN BLAKELY

Montlake
Romance

Text copyright © 2016 Lauren Blakely

Published by Montlake Romance, Seattle

www.apub.com

Amazon, the Amazon logo, and Montlake Romance are trademarks of Amazon.com, Inc., or its affiliates.

ISBN-13: 9781503935693
ISBN-10: 1503935698

Cover design by Michael Rehder

Cover photography by Regina Wamba of MaeIDesign.com

Printed in the United States of America

CHAPTER ONE

Steph wedged a fake ruby into the treasure chest, parking it next to a bright, gleaming emerald.

Fake, too.

Like Jake's feelings for her had been. Clearly.

Clenching her jaw, she fumed as she arranged the gaudy gems inside a plastic underwater treasure chest, her mind latching on to Jake's deception. She could barely believe the man had stolen so brazenly from her.

She placed one remaining bauble in the chest, then stood up. "It's a real pirate's bounty, arrr," she said, fixing on her pirate tone, trying desperately to cover up the cocktail of hurt and frustration roiling in her heart and head.

She gestured to the chest, her last bit of prep for the midmorning Stingray City Sandbar visit to kiss and pet the sea creatures.

Her deeply tanned, longtime Caymans friend Devon joined her in the corner of his snorkel shop. "Ah, but that's a beauty right there. Worth several thousand galleons," he said in a pirate voice, too.

Despite the plumes of anger licking her veins, she managed a small laugh. "I'll just go bury it in the sea now," she said, then grabbed the box, hoisted it up to her hip, and pushed open the door of his shop. She walked along the dock, set the treasure chest on the worn wood, then jumped into the shallow blue waters.

Ah, the ocean's caress felt good. But even it wasn't enough to numb the pain.

Carefully, she tugged the chest off the dock, into the water, and under the placid surface.

These phony gems were worth more than the contents of her hotel safe now that Jake had pilfered her very real diamond. Handsome, charming, no-good Jake. Her blood boiled as she thought about what he'd done last night. The man had actually broken into her safe—*again*—and taken her precious diamond after sleeping with her. That had probably been part of his nefarious plan. Drug her up on multiple orgasms so he could make off with her big rock.

Admittedly, he was a master at delivering *O*s.

But she could not, should not, would not let that lessen his crime. He'd stolen the one thing she owned that was worth something. She'd been planning on cashing it in and using the proceeds as a thank-you for her mom, who'd helped rebuild Steph's adventure tour business after her ex-boyfriend had tried to take it down.

So much for the gift.

She dragged the chest beneath the dock, then popped open the cover. The ten-cent fake gems glittered, like a pirate's booty. The customers would surely get a kick out of discovering this pretend treasure after they smooched the nearby stingrays. She popped up in the water, her hair sleek and wet, then took a breath and climbed onto the dock. She marched to the store, annoyance powering every step she took, her lips a tight, fierce line as she flicked back to last night with Jake when they'd stumbled into her room, flush with lust and desire, finally ready to give in to all that they'd felt.

The sex had been red-hot.

Out-of-this-world intense.

Butterflies had the audacity to swoop in her belly with the memory of how he'd touched her. She wanted to throat punch her traitorous hormones for longing for that cad of a man.

That damn pirate.

She couldn't believe that sometime in the middle of the night when she was sleeping, he'd actually sneaked out of bed, opened her safe, snagged her diamond, then took off with it after making love to her again as the dawn rose.

They'd even eaten breakfast together, and she'd shared with him the honey she liked so much. Such a little thing, but it was one more way she'd started to knock down her walls and let him into her guarded heart. She'd been played for a fool.

When she reached the screen door on the side of Devon's snorkel shop, she yanked it open, nearly ripping it off its hinges.

"Careful there," Devon warned.

"I will," she said, patting the door gently in apology, then fixing on her best chipper tone. "And everything's ready."

She had to set aside her ire, because it was business time. Her job was to show the customers a helluva good time in the water with the stingrays. She wasn't going to let a man get in the way of her work. She didn't trust men. She didn't trust love. She only trusted . . . well . . . fish. Fish were reliable; men were proving more vexing by the day. Ironic, since she'd hoped to learn the opposite on this trip. She'd come to the Caymans wanting to find a way to believe in the good in people, even when they were accused of bad, like her stepdad. But Jake's deception only confirmed that no matter how sentimental her heart became, she would be wise to listen to her brain.

Her brain said, *Don't trust.*

At least she had her work, though, and she loved her job madly.

Fifteen minutes later, a quartet of happily married sisters and their husbands arrived for a private stingray tour.

"Who wants to kiss a stingray and get lucky?" Steph said in a bright, upbeat tone as she and Devon escorted them into the shallow waters.

Funny how she'd gotten lucky last night, but it came with a price this morning.

A $10,000 one.

CHAPTER TWO

Jake dropped several coins in a copper offering plate as he entered the island church, which was thick with tropical scents from a sea of votive candles lining a long, low table.

Midmorning sun streaked through stained glass windows, casting jewel-toned rays of light across pews, white walls, and the wooden floorboards. The benches were dotted with a handful of visitors, heads bent in prayer.

He nodded silently, a sign of his respect for their studious contemplation, even though they couldn't see him. Unless they had eyes in the back of their heads, and nobody seemed to. On quiet feet, he walked to the staircase at the edge of the church entryway, then up the curving steps to the second floor of the house of worship. Windows stretched around the perimeter, giving it a light and airy feel.

The best part of the windows was the view they afforded—a clear shot into the art gallery across the street, wedged next to an empty storefront on one side and the Atlantis submarine tours on the other, with a slim alley slicing between the gallery and the vacant shop. That must be the property Isla and Eli were trying to purchase to expand the gallery.

Good Lord, business must be good in "Artlandia" if they had the kind of change needed to annex a shop. He chuckled to himself. Of course business was good for Eli. The man was a thief. The bastard stole money from hardworking Americans. Jake dug his fingers into his palms, a burst of righteous anger fueling him—a reminder of why he did what he did for a living. Because rich, privileged men like Eli Thompson thought nothing of skimming a little off the top. Eli had done that to the tune of $10 million from his very own hedge fund, stealing it from the Middle America customers the fund served. Then he turned their retirement savings to diamonds and skipped out of the good old USA and into the Caymans with the loot in his pockets, and Jake had the evidence to prove it, thanks to his client—that same fund. All he needed to do now was locate those watermarked diamonds, take them back, and return the money to its rightful owners.

Eli had gotten away with his fraud so far. But the road stopped here with Jake. His mantra was simple: "Don't let the bastards get away with anything."

That was the promise he'd made as a teenager after the drunk driver who smashed into his parents' car had gotten off scot-free. Now as an adult, Jake had no qualms whatsoever with tracking down the criminals and scum of the world to make sure they paid up.

Soon, it would be Eli's turn.

And if the tip he and Steph had garnered last night about the location of the gems was right—inside the frames on the art in the gallery office—Eli's opportunity to pay the piper was coming due any minute. Made sense that the rocks would be stuffed inside frames. You could store a lot of stones in that sort of clever hiding spot. Come to think of it, the frames he'd seen in the halls at Eli's Sapphire nightclub had an unusual look to them, too. Strangely heavy for such light, contemporary art. One more possible option to pursue.

Jake lowered his shades, placed his palms on the windowsill, and stared across the street. From the second story of the church, he had a bird's-eye view of the gallery. Well, it was really courtesy of the binoculars built into the awesome sunglasses he wore today that he was able to keep watch on the back door, then the front, then the alley along the side of Isla's Island Gallery. The most useful sunglasses ever, they provided a close-up look into what was many feet away. He enjoyed the little gadgets of the job, like his lock-picking kit and the sunglasses with the built-in zoom.

With its bright white walls and steel framework, the gallery exuded class and style. The proprietor was catering to the wealthiest clientele on the island, even if it was located amid souvenir shops, bars, and tour operators. As Jake scanned the swank location, he took mental note of the number of employees visible in the gallery—three, including one at the reception desk—as well as the activity of the establishment.

Busy.

A green Honda pulled up outside the gallery, and a tall guy with graying hair emerged, glanced at the gallery doorway, then popped into a souvenir shop down the block. A thick, burly man in a suit strolled by next, ducking into the gallery for five minutes or so, chatting with Isla the whole time. A woman in a flowy red dress walked in next.

When the woman left the gallery, she blew a kiss to Isla, who held open the door. The woman breezed down the street with a brochure in hand. Jake checked his watch. One more hour 'til showtime. This morning in Steph's hotel room, they'd checked out every angle of Isla's Island Gallery with Google street view as they'd prepped, but it was wise to obtain an actual visual with one's own eyes.

Though the visual he wanted in his line of sight again was Steph Anderson.

Beautiful, blonde, athletic, clever, witty, *pain-in-the-ass-and-he-loved-it* Steph Anderson. The woman who swam with turtles, who loved her family, and who kissed with passion and fell apart in his arms.

As he stared across the street, he adjusted his shorts. Just the memory of her up against the wall, then beneath him, then straddling him, sent bolts of lust through his groin. Last night with her blew his mind and torched all the pathways in his body. She gave herself to him in all the ways that he wanted, and he couldn't wait to have his hands on her again.

But he also wanted the rest of those damn diamonds that he was sure were inside that gallery.

Wanted them badly. His fingers itched to touch them.

He patted his pocket, running his thumb along the outline of a little something he'd taken from Steph's hotel this morning. He chuckled silently at the memory of lifting this sweet object. It had been so easy—taking candy from a baby, for sure.

He only hoped snagging Eli's diamonds would be as smooth. Once he had his hands on all those blue-tinted beauties, he'd be good to go. He could get the hell out of Dodge and head on home to Key Largo. See his sister, see his nephew, have a brew with his buddy Dan. Maybe even fish off the dock near his house.

But out of nowhere, a pang lurched in his heart as he pictured boarding a plane and leaving this island. He scratched his head. *What was that all about?* He was ready to be done with this job today, thank you very much.

Except if he finished it, he'd have to say good-bye to Steph.

No reason for him to be missing her.

They were only having a tropical affair, a little island tryst. Besides, neither one had time for anything more than the here and now. Once he was gone, he'd need to zero in on whatever was coming his way next. Not linger on the woman he wouldn't see again. Get her out of his mind.

But as he ran a hand absently over his chin, it occurred to him that maybe this odd feeling inside him wasn't so unusual, considering Steph was sweet, feisty, smart, game for adventure, and had a vulnerability in her that latched onto his heart. They had a damn good time together— he made her laugh, and she did the same for him.

His lips curved up in a grin as he thought of her. He shrugged happily to himself. Fine, if the job lasted a few more days, that wasn't so bad. He'd been lucky so far. Getting involved with her had only helped him on this case. She'd been a great partner, and they were that much closer to cracking it because of her. He rapped his knuckles soundlessly against the windowsill—knocking wood that his lucky streak would continue. He could see spending time with her, chartering a fishing boat for an afternoon maybe, casting away far from shore, lolling about on the open sea. Naturally, the fantasy boat trip would include screwing on the deck of the boat. Many, many times. The image of her legs wrapped around his hips as he took her under the sun burned into his brain.

Hell, he'd stay extra on the island to make that happen. He'd definitely extend his trip for that sort of quality time.

The clacking of shoes echoed in his ears and snapped him out of his daydream. Glancing briefly behind him, he caught sight of a man in slacks and a dark short-sleeve shirt adorned with a name tag bearing the name of the church. The man looked at Jake and flashed a brief smile.

"If there is anything you need, let me know," he said with a bow.

"Of course. Beautiful church you have," Jake said.

"Do you need help getting down the stairs?"

Jake furrowed his brow. Why on earth would he need help down the steps? Did he look feeble? As he scrunched up his nose, it hit him why the man had asked. Jake was wearing dark glasses indoors. The man thought he was blind.

He laughed quietly and shook his head. "I'm all good," he said. With sunglasses still covering his eyes, he headed down the steps, figuring it was best not to linger, even in a place where everyone was welcoming.

As he weaved past the table of pineapple and coconut candles, he reached into his pocket, grabbed his wallet, and opened it. He fished around for some bills—time to up his donation. This church had been good to him. He left a few on the donation plate, then pushed on the bright white door.

A blast of warm air blanketed him.

His phone rang. Taylor Swift. Grabbing the phone from his pocket, he turned in the opposite direction of the gallery, threading his way through late-morning tourists, shopping and strolling along the street, as he answered his little sister's call. He braced himself for more bad news about her grades.

"Hey, Kylie. Are you a physics wiz now? Running experiments left and right in the school's science lab?"

His sister moaned.

Uh-oh.

"Not yet. I have to take summer school first," she said.

"For physics?"

"The school said even with a tutor, I won't have the science requirements to finish unless I take summer classes. I need the tutor *and* summer school."

"Then we'll get you into summer school," he said, keeping his tone upbeat for her sake, even though summer school meant more bills. Law school tuition would be coming due soon for Brandt, and now he had more classes to pony up for. But getting Kylie and Brandt through school was his mission, and he was glad he could support his family, even if it meant busting his ass and working all the time. It also meant he'd need to find another gig quickly once this one wrapped up. *If* it wrapped up. "How's the tutor? Is he helping?"

"So much," she said, then sighed, the contented sound of a Disney princess after she's caught a glimpse of Prince Charming. His radar went off before she even said the next words.

"He is so handsome. I think I might be in love with him already."

Jake cringed as he walked past an ice-cream shop. "Let's not jump the gun on the romance, Kylie. Let's focus on the schoolwork."

"I know. I will. But it doesn't hurt that he's dreamy."

Jake shook his head, cursing himself for having picked a tutor she wound up crushing on. Next time, he'd need to hire a nun to teach her science, because now he had to get his little sister to focus on school again, not boys. Some days, it was exhausting taking care of her and doing his best to surrogate parent her from afar. He wondered what his dad would say. How his mom would handle this. What would they do when the baby of the family wound up distracted by boys? He wished he knew, but it was now up to him and his oldest sister, Kate, to make sure the younger kids made their way safely into adulthood.

"I'm sure it doesn't, but let's talk physics. Tell me what's going on," he said firmly, refocusing her on the task at hand.

"I have a test tomorrow. The tutor is going to study with me this afternoon, so I'm hoping that'll help."

"Yeah, me, too. But listen, Kylie. You can't just stare into his eyes and let him hypnotize you with hotness. That's not going to help."

"You're one to talk. How's your island hottie?" she asked, needling him as only she could.

"I have no idea what you're talking about," he said with pretend stoicism.

"Ha. Deny all you want. You can't fool me."

"Never could," he muttered playfully. "Back to you. You're going to focus on studying, 'K?"

"I will. I promise," she said, and Jake knew his little sister was trying, but hell, she was trying him, too.

But that was just the way it was. She was his complicated girl, and it was his job to see her through. That's what his dad would have done. When he finished with Kylie, he checked his screen to see if Steph had tried to contact him. Then he rolled his eyes at his own pathetic actions and promptly reprimanded himself. He was seeing her in an hour. He could totally wait. He needn't act like some lovesick fool, staring at his screen to see if his woman called.

His woman?

He smacked the side of his own head.

Get it together.

Last night was just sex.

Steph was just fun.

Their time together was only temporary. She was not *his*.

He shoved the phone into his pocket, and the metal case clanged against metal. Hitting the edge of the little trinket he'd lifted from her hotel. He didn't want anything to happen to that goodie.

CHAPTER THREE

"The ruby is gorgeous. It looks so real!"

Splash.

"Check out the emerald. I wonder what a real one that size would be worth."

Rubber fins slapped the crystal-blue waters as a pair of curly-haired sisters from the quartet of thirtysomething couples in the stingray group freestyled their way to the treasure chest. The chest gleamed with fake riches under the dock, fifteen feet away from where Steph and Devon dug their toes into the sand and watched the couples in their private tour group having a blast.

Steph bumped a wet fist with Devon. Their customers were getting a kick out of the make-believe treasure. The two women pretended to paw at it as they neared the box of oversize fake gems, the kind of chest that would fit right at home inside a fish tank.

"Never gets old," Devon mused.

"Wouldn't it be something to really find a chest full of jewels in the sea," Steph said as the sun warmed her shoulders and deepened her tan. "Maybe even diamonds. Maybe modern-day swashbuckling pirates are hiding all their jewels here in the ocean."

She wished the hunt for the diamonds were as easy as making a beeline underwater for gems. Grabbing them, taking them home to Miami, converting them to cash, and repaying those whose accounts had been skimmed. Now she had to grapple with mounting evidence against her stepdad, as well as her own frayed hope that someone else was behind all those e-mails that seemed to damn him. Maybe even Isla. The only way to find out was to find the jewels.

"Buried treasure is just an old wives' tale," Devon said quietly.

"I know. I just wish sometimes it were true," she whispered, fiddling with her treasure chest necklace that her mom had made for her, remembering the night Jake had brushed the pads of his fingers against it as they'd walked on the beach and she'd told him about her parents—about the father she never knew and her deep and abiding love for her mom. She shivered from the memory of how sweet his words were that evening, how gentle his touch. A sad wistfulness descended on her. She'd really liked the guy. He'd been fun and forthright, witty and sharp, and caring. He'd had such a wonderful heart . . . or so it seemed until he stole her diamond this morning, even though some of the messy details of the theft nagged at her brain.

She chased away thoughts of him as the sisters admired the gleaming blue sapphire at the top of the pile of gems. The sister in the purple bikini grabbed a fake rock.

"Everyone loves a sapphire," the purple-bikini sister declared as she held up a huge blue rock, the sun glinting off its surface. "I've never understood why diamonds are worth more. These are much more stunning." She gazed intently at the phony gem, studying it from all angles.

"It's so gorgeous," the other one chimed in. "It looks priceless."

"It does," the purple-bikini sister said.

Steph straightened her spine, awareness zipping through her. That simple action of holding the sapphire reminded Steph to keep her eye on the prize.

Sapphire. Eli. Diamonds. Money.

She needed to stop alternating between anger and sadness over Jake. This trip was never about a man. It was about a mission—a chance to right a wrong. She was meeting Jake in less than an hour, and she had to figure out how to play the angles with him. Not moon over what might have been. Besides, this was all for the best. She was at odds with Jake, and her brain had known all along to keep a distance from him.

Twenty minutes later, she and Devon said good-bye to the group from the doorway of the snorkel shop.

"Hope you enjoyed your time in the water," Devon said.

"We had an amazing morning. The stingrays alone were worth the trip, but you made it so much fun with the treasure chest," the purple-bikini sister said as she fastened a tie around her wet hair.

"Here. Take the sapphire," Steph said with a smile, placing the bright-blue stone in the woman's hand when she finished knotting her strands.

The lady clutched the rock to her chest as if it were a true prize. "I'll take it back to Idaho and say I uncovered it in the Stingray City Sandbar," she said, then waved as they departed.

Steph set to work straightening up the shop and putting away gear on the shelves. "Thanks again for letting me do the tour with you," she said to her buddy. Her own tour started in three more days. She was guiding a group of tourists on a dive through some of the nearby wrecks not far from shore, then out on a longer excursion dive to Little Cayman, sixty miles away. There, on the north side of the island, were some of the best dive spots in the world, including the Bloody Bay site with a wall so deep it was nearly vertical, making for a spectacular dive. She loved that spot and couldn't wait to visit it again.

"My pleasure. I told you you're a good-luck charm. One of the guys in the group said he's already told some friends who are coming here next month that they need to do our stingray tour."

Steph's eyes lit up. If there was one true thing that was priceless, it was positive word-of-mouth. She punched Devon on the biceps. "That is awesome."

"They said how much fun you were, too, with the jewels," he added as he grabbed mesh bags of gear.

She beamed as she tucked the snorkels away in the storage room. "Well, that pretty much makes my day."

"I found his comment all the more amazing considering I'm pretty sure you were pissed about something before the tour started. You did a good job, though, focusing on the customers," he said, arching an eyebrow and waiting for her to pick up the baton of the deeper conversation. "What's on your mind, Steph?"

She sighed. Shrugged. Fiddled with her hair. Then bit the bullet. "What would you do if you suspected someone you liked took something from you, but you weren't entirely sure. Would you confront that person?"

"Whoa." He held up his hands. "That's a loaded question if I ever heard one."

"I know," she said with a heavy sigh as she adjusted a mask neatly next to some fins.

"Care to tell me more? So I can help?"

She pursed her lips, rewinding to the last few days with Jake. "I'm not sure where to start."

But the truth was, she didn't want to say the words out loud—*Did the guy I slept with steal the diamond my stepfather bought with stolen money in the first place?* Nope. She couldn't breathe those words aloud. She didn't want either the front or the back end of that statement to be true.

This was a mystery best solved solo, so she finished her work, packed up, and headed to her Jeep, still noodling on the details.

Jake was a professional. He cracked safes and covered his tracks for a living, so why was the safe left open? Wouldn't he assume she'd check her safe? He wasn't sloppy; she'd learned that much about him. The man had amazing follow-through, both on the job and in bed.

Still, he'd stayed in her room all night. Hell, he'd asked, damn near insisted on spending the night, and he knew how to break into a safe. She just wasn't sure why he'd done it the way he had. Maybe to throw her off the scent? Make it seem like someone else had broken into the safe?

She burned with frustration.

How was she to proceed with him? Business as usual or full inquisition?

As she pulled on the handle of the auto, she stole one last look at the calm blue water, teeming with friendly stingrays. An oxymoron.

But in it, she found the answer.

Stingrays sounded scary.

After all, who wants to be stung? But rather than fear them, tourists kissed them.

Steph would glean more answers with honey than vinegar. Confronting Jake about stealing the diamond would only give him a greater chance to backpedal. She'd need to act like nothing was amiss. She wouldn't let on that she suspected he was a thief.

Keep your friends close and your enemies closer.

CHAPTER FOUR

She looked good.

But then, that seemed to be the woman's specialty.

Being stunning. Being hot. Being the sun-kissed beauty he was damn lucky to spend a little time with.

As she walked down the block, all he could think about was smothering her in kisses. Cupping her face in his hands, gazing into her gorgeous blue eyes, lacing his fingers through that blonde hair. Maybe even tugging on it.

Did she like hair pulling?

Note to self: find out if Steph enjoys hair pulling, spanking, and playful biting.

She wore an aqua-green sundress with some kind of swirly pattern. He intended to take it off her. Soon. Very soon. But first they had business to do. Catered lunch to order. A mission to accomplish. He sat outside at a café a few blocks away from the gallery. A Frommer's guidebook was open on the table, adding to the tourist look he'd perfected.

When Steph reached the table, she shot him a sultry stare that scorched him. With her mere inches away, his earlier wish for the case to end quickly vanished into thin air. Let the case drag on. Let the diamonds go unfound for a few more days. He wanted time with her. To get to know her better, her body and her mind.

But the voice of reason told him the more he gave in, the more he risked. Only, he wasn't thinking with reason right now. He wasn't thinking at all. Only feeling how much he longed for this woman.

"Good afternoon, gorgeous mermaid," he said, his voice dry and husky.

"Flattery will get you everywhere," she said with a wink, then parked herself on his lap and threw her arms around him.

"Good to see you, too," he said with a chuckle.

She clasped his face in her hands and purred. "I missed you this morning." Her voice turned to a feathery whisper. "I can't wait to have you inside me again."

Oh Lord.

The woman didn't mince words.

His dick shot straight up, and he was grateful she was on his lap, covering his hard-on. He was even more grateful that she claimed his mouth in a heady kiss. She pressed her lips to his; the taste of her was so damn sweet. He nearly groaned in pleasure, a sound that would've been wholly inappropriate in public company.

He slipped his tongue inside her warm mouth, and his brain went hazy. All thoughts of work, and tutors, and summer school, and jobs, and whatever else he needed to do crumbled to dust in the caress of her lips. She kissed like a dream, and he could get lost in these kisses, in this sweet, feisty, fiery woman.

He let himself for a minute or two, as her hot kisses blurred out the world.

But in the back of his mind the clock ticked loudly. As much as it pained him, he broke the kiss. "One, that was epic. Two, I want more. Three, I've been thinking about you all morning."

"I've been thinking of you, too," she said, running her fingers along the front of his shirt. She smiled at him, a grin that spread from sea to shining sea. She was happy today. Wildly happy, and it was infectious.

"You're cuddly today."

She shrugged coyly, then brushed a finger along his jawline. "I guess the best sex of my life makes me that way. Hope you don't mind," she said, pursing her lips playfully. She sneaked a hand behind him and gripped his ass. Squeezed it hard.

He hitched in a breath. "Now listen, sexy girl, you're going to send me into the gallery with a hard-on if we keep this up."

"But I like you hard," she said, gripping the fabric of his shirt. Her hands were everywhere. Zipping all over him. Grabbing him. Touching him. Like an attack of fantastic sensations.

"It's a state I vastly enjoy being in when I'm with you. But I do work better when I'm not thinking about fucking you," he said, then lifted her off him, and they left the busy café and turned to a side street away from the crowds.

"Ready to place the order?" he said, then ducked down a quiet block along the beach.

She reached for her phone from her bag, blocked her number, and made the phone call.

They needed to get inside Isla's gallery to look around. Nighttime would have been ideal, but there was simply too much security in the evenings in this section of town. Stores, restaurants, and high-end hotels nearby employed ample guards after hours, so they'd have to find a way to get into Isla's office during the day.

Their plan was risky but far safer than breaking in after hours, when they stood a good chance of being caught and hauled away. They had to get inside during the day, when no one suspected a break-in.

As Steph called, Jake crossed his fingers, hoping all the pieces fell into place.

"Good afternoon. This is Clementine's Catering," the woman who answered the phone said in a cheery voice.

As a palm tree swayed gently in the breeze by the water, Steph adopted her best professional tone. "Hi there. This is Lynx O'Malley's personal assistant. We spoke earlier when I placed an order for lunch."

"Yes, indeed. How can I help you? This is Clementine."

"Ah, wonderful. Good to chat with you, Clementine. I'm calling to confirm the lunch delivery to Isla's Island Gallery. It will be there in twenty minutes, correct?" Steph asked, pushing her sunglasses up on the bridge of her nose. Earlier that day, during the morning planning session with Jake at her hotel, they'd come up with the plan—it was a distraction strategy, but Steph hoped it would work long enough to sniff around. All they needed was to buy some time in the daylight, when no one would suspect what they were up to.

Steph had placed the order, supposedly on behalf of Isla's favorite artist, who was on a meditation retreat. Steph had paid for the pending lunch delivery with an American Express gift card, so she remained untraceable.

"Yes, ma'am. We pride ourselves on on-time delivery," Clementine said, sounding as peppy as her name. "One p.m. sharp. We've got the beet salad, the cucumber sandwiches, the mushroom caviar—"

"And the olives?"

"Indeed, we have the olives."

Jake stood next to her, an eager look in his wide-open eyes. She flashed him a thumbs-up, like she genuinely wanted to reassure him that everything was on track between the two of them. He grinned in return. Fabulous. He had no clue she was on to his ruse.

"And you'll be sure to stay and serve all the food?" Steph said, returning to her phone call and resuming her pace along the street, Jake by her side. "I ask because Lynx wants Isla and her staff to feel treated to a wonderful meal as a special way of saying thank you for all the amazing work she's done for the art community," Steph said with a flourish in her tone.

"In my humble opinion, nothing quite says thank you like specialty olives and roasted beet salad."

"Excellent. Lynx is so thrilled. He can't wait to hear how much she enjoys the gourmet catered lunch," Steph said, thinking that Lynx wouldn't even know he'd sent them lunch for a few more days. She suspected he wasn't tied to his phone while on a retreat. They walked past a sandwich shop boasting Caribbean-themed panini served on the patio under a red-checked awning. They smelled yummy, and the scent reminded her that some nourishment would be mighty welcome in her belly. But there'd be time for that later.

Now it was work work work.

Steph hung up and smiled at the enemy. Her plan was working. The man was putty in her arms, and once they pulled off Mission Lunch, she'd pull off Get Back My Damn Diamond. "All systems are go."

❀

"Let's review this," Jake said, parking his hands on her shoulders as they stood outside the panini shop. To get her to focus, but also because he liked touching her.

"Yes, let's review everything," she said, that same sexy tone returning to her voice. She was a live wire of sexuality today.

"If you see something or hear something, or if they start to move, you text me. It's set to buzz when you call," he said, letting go of one shoulder to tap his back pocket where his phone was parked.

"Let's hope I don't have to buzz you . . . unless it's for me wanting you," she said, her voice smooth like honey.

Honey. Funny that he thought of honey just now.

He bent his head closer to her, brushed a kiss along her neck. "You are driving me wild today," he said with a groan. "But we need to get into position."

"I can think of some positions I'd like," she said, slipping her hands around his back, then down to his butt. For the briefest moment, she almost seemed to be patting his back pockets. Maybe she was reassuring herself that his phone was there. She probably wanted to know he was highly reachable if need be.

"As can I. But let's save all that for later. I promise as soon as we finish today, I will be giving you a well-deserved trio of your favorite things," he said as he extracted himself from her grip. He tipped his forehead to the sandwich shop. "And taking you there for lunch if you want. I think the look in your eyes says you're lusting after a panini."

"No. Just you," she said, all flirty and dirty.

He resisted. Didn't take the bait this time. "You'll need these," he said as he reached for his shades. Her gaze was fixed on his hand taking the binoculars from his pocket. He flicked them open and placed them on her face.

"Ooh, I feel like James Bond now."

He explained how they worked, where she should station herself in the church, and his expected timeframe. "You'll be safe there in the church. No one will know you're involved."

"Don't you get yourself caught," she warned.

He saluted her. "I'm like a cat. No one will hear me. My job is to be invisible," he said, then made a *poof* gesture with his hands.

Twenty minutes later, they were in their locations, Steph watching the gallery through the church window, while Jake ambled along the street, checking out souvenirs of seashells at a shop kitty corner to the gallery. As he pretended to consider a conch shell keychain, a white Subaru with an image of an orange painted on the door pulled up and parked.

He set the keychain on its holder, left the shop, and strolled casually toward the gallery.

A woman in chef whites emerged from the Subaru, yanked open the hatchback, and grabbed a tray full of gourmet food. Jake smiled to himself as she headed to Isla's Island Gallery.

A lunch ambush.

Nothing won people over faster than food. A free meal was, quite simply, a top trick of the trade, and one of the best methods of distraction known to mankind. If all went as planned, lunch would provide enough momentary cover for him to slip in through the back door. There were never any guarantees on ploys and decoys, but gifts of food usually granted you at least five minutes of safe cover while everyone converged on the goodies at once. Like animals guarding a meal, most people wouldn't walk away from a delicious lunch spread.

As he neared the entrance to the gallery, he trained his ears on the conversation in the doorway as Clementine walked up the steps.

The black-haired Isla cocked her head to the side as the caterer spoke.

"Good afternoon. I'm Clementine from Clementine's Catering here on Grand Cayman Island. I have a surprise lunch delivery for Isla and her amazing staff from Mr. Lynx O'Malley," the caterer said, and Isla made an excited *ooh* sound. Clementine continued. "He wanted to send you this delicious gourmet lunch to thank you for all the hard work you put forth in representing his art and selling it."

Isla's eyes widened, and she waved Clementine inside. "How wonderful! Lynx is the most thoughtful artist I've ever worked with."

Once the caterer crossed the threshold, Jake darted into the alley, made a beeline for the back door, and quickly wriggled it open. The task took less than forty seconds. Not quite a personal best, but damn close. He held his breath and said a quick prayer.

Keep them busy. Don't let me be seen. Let me find the diamonds.

Quietly, he opened the door and peered around. Down the narrow hall. Toward the restroom. Then the *X* marked the spot—Isla's office. Bam.

As he listened for the sounds of culinary delight in the main room—lip smacking, oohing and aahing—he opened the door, left it ajar, and spun in a circle in her office.

There was no art.

There were no frames.

The walls were bare.

CHAPTER FIVE

He was inside.

So easily.

Because that's what he did. Slipped in and out and stole.

She was damn near ready to just let him dangle.

Hang him out to dry.

Hell, he was probably going to do the same to her. But the only way to uncover his true intention, and potentially the jewels, was to stick to the plan. That meant she was wearing his zoom lens shades and staring out a stained glass window in a Cayman Islands house of worship.

She had to give the guy credit. He'd tracked down a great lookout point and was doing the dirty work. He was the one putting himself in the line of fire. He could get caught red-handed with the jewels; that was the risk with this lunch ploy, but it was the only way. She had to run lookout because Isla, or one of her two employees, might wander to the back office any second, peek around a doorframe, and spot Jake lifting the diamonds.

Lifting the diamonds.

Lifting the diamonds.

Lifting the diamonds.

The words echoed like a gong.

Holy shit. He'd said he wanted her to be safe, but instead he'd cleverly shoved her out of his way. With her in the church across the street, he was scot-free to waltz away with *all* the diamonds now. Every single last one of them.

She was a world-class idiot. But it wasn't too late to abort and restart.

Her blood pumped fast and hard. Her brain went into overdrive. Time for a new plan. He'd taken one diamond. If he found the others, he'd likely stuff them into his pocket and jet straight out of town. She'd have nothing in her hands to try to prove Eli's innocence, though that was less likely. Still, if she had the diamonds, she could try like hell to convince her stepdad to do the right thing. She could help exonerate him. She'd tried talking sense into him, and he hadn't listened.

But she'd have no chance of doing that if Jake beat her to the punch. She was not going to be screwed over once again by a man she trusted.

She huffed and turned around, coming face-to-face with a gentleman in slacks and a button-down. She flinched. She hadn't expected to see anyone. But she breathed easier when his name tag indicated he worked at the church.

"Hello. Do you need anyone to pray with?" he asked, hands pressed together, bowing slightly.

"No," she said through gritted teeth. "But it would be great if you can pray for mercy for Jake. Thanks so much."

She practically vaulted her way to the stairwell, down the steps, and out the main door.

The new plan took shape in seconds, because that was all the time she had. She'd have to improvise, but her one supposed drawback—that people knew her in this town—was her one advantage. Steph could infiltrate. She could head straight into the gallery. Isla liked her, and Isla would probably insist she stay.

Have some beets. Enjoy some olives. Here's some coconut flan.

She hightailed it to the gallery, pushing her shades up on her head. No need for the spy gear. She was invited, because she was always welcome. Privilege of being the stepdaughter, and she'd gladly take it now. She grabbed the handle of the gallery door, tugged it open, and entered a scene of art, laughter, and a smorgasbord of food she'd ordered with an untraceable gift card.

Steph waved, acting casual. "Just in the neighborhood. Wanted to say hi."

Isla's chocolate brown eyes lit up. She wore a sleek, short cranberry dress and her dark hair was curled in waves that fell on her shoulders. "So good to see you, Steph. You came by at the perfect time."

"I did?" Steph asked, feigning surprise. "Lucky me."

"Yes. Look at all our food," Isla said, beaming as she gestured to the trays of food the caterer had set up. Isla promptly introduced her to the two employees and the caterer, and Steph hoped Clementine wouldn't recognize her voice from the phone call.

Isla clutched her arm. "Can you join us? It's such a treat to see you again. Come, have some beets and olives and we'll discuss the amazing generosity of my favorite artist in the world, Lynx O'Malley. He sent this special lunch to us, and I can show you some of his art on the walls," she said, gesturing proudly to the bright white walls adorned with his images. "And we can talk and catch up properly."

"I would love to," Steph said, though she had no intention of partaking in a tour. She gestured in the general direction of the back hallway, then lowered her voice. "I'm just going to pop into the ladies' room first. Be right back."

Isla parted her lips to speak, probably to offer to show Steph where the restroom was. But that was not going to fly. Steph might be pissed at Jake, but she didn't want him to be caught. She spun efficiently on her heels and walked to the rear of the gallery, crossing her fingers that the trays of yummy food would continue to distract Isla and her employees.

She turned the corner in the hallway, safe from the front of the shop. The food had worked its charm, rooting hungry humans to the trays, just as she and Jake had hoped it would.

Steph yanked open the office door.

Jake stood at the desk with some papers in his hand. She wanted to shout, "Busted!" but opted for a closed-mouth smile.

He furrowed his brow. *Everything OK?* he mouthed.

"No," she whispered. "Get the diamonds and let's go."

"They're not here," he said quietly with a shrug.

Like she believed that.

"It's not safe," she said, then tipped her head to the door. "Go."

Nodding crisply, he folded the paper, stuffed it into his pocket, and followed her lead as she shoved him down the hall and into the alley.

"What's going on?" he asked quietly.

She shook her head. Kept her lips closed. Patted him down. Ran her hands along his sides. He squirmed and laughed.

She fought back a grin. "Ticklish much?"

"Suspicious much?" he tossed back. "Seriously, what are you doing? Not that I mind your hands on me, but something tells me you aren't trying to cop a feel."

"I am. I really am. I can't keep my hands off you," she said, trying valiantly to maintain her act as she reached into one shorts pocket, then the other. Her fingers brushed across a small glass object. Her spine tingled, and she arched an eyebrow. It felt like a jam jar. "Did you put the diamonds in a jam jar?"

He shook his head. "No. That's a gift. But now it's ruined," he said with a huff.

She didn't have time to process this comment as she patted his shirt pocket. They were all empty except for his wallet, phone, and the folded-up piece of paper. Fine, this was promising. For the most part.

"Why are you acting like I'm taking something, then?" he asked skeptically, with narrowed eyes.

"I'm not," she said, fixing on an oh-so-sweet smile. "I was just eager to get my hands on you, and the diamonds. But there really weren't any diamonds in there? I saw that the walls were bare."

He held up his hands, as if he were solemnly swearing. "I didn't find any. I have no clue how Penny got that tip, but it was inaccurate. There wasn't even a single frame on the wall. I did find some interesting paperwork, though, about some donations—"

She pressed her finger to his lips. "Shh. I need to go excuse myself from this rendezvous so Isla doesn't think I'm cuckoo. Then tell me all about the paperwork." She tugged on Jake's shirt. "You need to wait by the souvenir shop."

He nodded but furrowed his brow. "You're acting strange. And a little bossy."

"It's a full moon," she said quickly. Jake left the alley before her and headed to the souvenir shop. While he checked out some postcards, Steph doubled back to the door and then into the gallery again, where Isla's employees were praising the coconut flan. Her heart raced during those few moments, hoping he wouldn't escape. But she had to take this risk of zipping back the way she came or Isla might be suspicious of her. *How do burglars and career jewel thieves pull this off?* Managing a reverse con was no walk in the park.

Steph tapped Isla on the shoulder and motioned for her to come to the entryway. She'd have Jake in her line of sight that way. Steph breathed easier when she spotted the back of Jake's head and his golden-brown hair. "I hate to do this, but I just got a last-minute call to do a snorkel lesson for some beginners over at Happy Turtle, so I can't stay," Steph said, apologizing.

Isla frowned. "Oh no. I was looking forward to showing you the art. Can you come back?"

"I'll try," Steph said, casting her gaze briefly in Jake's direction. He thumbed through trinkets on display street side, milling about in place. Steph breathed more easily. He could have been running away, absconding with more jewels. But he was staying. Maybe he wasn't a total liar.

Which made her theories about what happened this morning even cloudier.

Steph returned her full attention to Isla, then jerked her head in surprise when she spotted something missing from Isla's wardrobe. Steph brought her fingers to her throat. Touching her own necklace. "Isla," she whispered, pointing to the other woman's neck. "What happened to your diamond? Is it being resized or something?"

Isla sighed heavily and clasped her hand over her heart. A pendant dangled from her neck, but it was missing the blue-tinted gem she'd worn at her house party. In its place was a too-bright cubic zirconium. A substitute rock.

Isla dropped her voice to a barren whisper. *"Stolen."*

Tension shot through Steph's bones. She furrowed her brow. "Are you serious? When? Where?"

"Last night. Right here," Isla said, pointing to the blond wood floors of the gallery. "During a reception. It was on my neck, then it was gone. I was freshening up my drink, and moments later, Eli noticed it was missing. It must have fallen out of the casing on the necklace, and then someone took it."

Steph blinked. She swallowed. Her skull echoed. "Right here? In the gallery? Last night? What time?"

"It was around eight."

Steph calculated. Jake was with her then on the boat. He couldn't have taken Isla's stone. "We looked everywhere. We canvassed the entire place," Isla continued, sweeping her hands around to indicate the enormity of the search.

"But how do you know it was stolen and not just misplaced?"

"We looked everywhere," Isla said. "As you can see, there isn't a lot of clutter. It's quite bare. But there was no diamond anywhere. So it can't have been lost."

"Do you have any idea who took it?"

"None. But thank God we moved the other diamonds from here a while ago."

The other diamonds.

Holy moly. Steph's jaw dropped. Clanged on the floor.

Isla admitted it. Officially. They had diamonds. Shock reverberated in her bones. But was Isla actually saying the gallery had once been the home for their diamond stash? "You had diamonds here?" she asked, pointing to the floor, trying to make sense of this new wrinkle.

Isla nodded. She placed a hand on Steph's back, lowering her voice more. "We used to have a lot here, but not anymore. You can't be too careful with precious stones. As you know, since Eli gave you one. I do hope you're keeping it safe. As safe as can be."

"Yes," Steph croaked out. She had no clue what else to say. No notion what to do. This new slew of information was slamming her around, knocking her left and right, like a cartoon character being pummeled and seeing stars. She tapped her wrist once more. "I should go."

"Let's do this another time," Isla said, her tone immediately jettisoning back to the fully upbeat woman Steph had briefly gotten to know.

She nearly stumbled out of the gallery, her breath coming fast, her blood racing through her veins.

Jake leaned against the brick wall of the souvenir shop, right where she'd told him to wait.

Was she wrong in her assumption that Jake had taken her gem?

Maybe he really didn't have the diamonds from the gallery. Perhaps Isla was telling the truth, and Eli moved them to a new location a while ago. Her head swam with possibilities, with far too many permutations. She needed to regroup, but she also needed to figure out if Jake was playing her.

And there was only one way to find out.

CHAPTER SIX

Get him naked.

Not to check body cavities. Because . . . eww.

But for another reason.

Because she hardly knew which way was up anymore. She wanted to trust Jake, so very badly. But she didn't know how to. She'd trusted Duke for years and was slapped in the face by him when their love went sour. She'd known Jake for less than a week. This was the man gunning for her stepdad. She had to be certain, beyond a reasonable doubt, that he wasn't playing her, and the only way to be certain was to conduct a thorough check of his clothes.

But first, the Novocain of a kiss.

The second the door to her room shut, she pounced on him, kissing hard to silence all conversation, to use the same drug on him that he'd used on her last night. Closeness. Connection. Red-hot contact. It had worked wonders at turning her into a quivering one-track woman, hell-bent only on pleasure. Maybe it could do the same to Jake so he'd easily let her investigate . . . his pockets.

As she consumed his lips, her brain whirred fast and crazy with a Rubik's Cube of possibilities.

He'd stolen the diamond while she was sleeping.

He hadn't stolen it at all.

Both Isla and Jake were lying about the jewels.

Jake was hiding the diamonds he'd taken from Isla's office.

In his shoe. In his wallet. In the pocket of his underwear.

Wait. Did underwear have pockets anymore? Did they ever have pockets?

What if maybe he wasn't hiding them at all?

There were too many outcomes, and she hardly knew how to navigate this topsy-turvy maze. As she slid her tongue between Jake's soft, delicious lips, her mind settled, and her body took the driver's seat. Kissing him intoxicated her, too. It had from the very first night. His kisses were preludes. A hint of what might come. An appetizer inviting her to the table of all the pleasure this man could give. She hummed with desire as she explored his mouth. Her skin sizzled and her belly flipped. Then it flopped again as he groaned from her kissing. A sexy, masculine rumble because of her, and how she took the reins and led this carnal moment.

He liked it, and dammit, so did she.

It both pissed her off and ignited her. In mere seconds of their lips sealing, she was wildly aroused when she wanted to feel nothing for him. Nothing but anger. Only, she felt so much more than nothing, especially because the Rubik's Cube of options was lining up squares in his favor as he looped his hands through her hair, then broke the kiss momentarily to whisper, "I have no idea why you're acting so strange today, but when you kiss me like that, I kind of stop caring." His voice was both husky and true. "I like it too much."

Her heart slammed to the ground, then bounced back up. She gave herself a pep talk.

Do it.

Checking would be for the best. She had to know, and there was one way to find out. Finish what she'd started outside the gallery and conduct her investigation.

"I like it, too," she said in a sexy purr, then dropped her lips to his neck, kissing a trail up his skin, savoring the clean scent of him, how he gripped her hair harder as she kissed, then nipped on his earlobe.

He groaned.

She flicked her tongue against the shell of his ear.

He grabbed her harder, crushing her body against his, his erection pressing into her.

Fuck, she wanted him.

The angel popped up on her shoulder. *Trust him.*

The devil appeared. *Frisk him.*

Before she could hesitate, she spoke in a rush. "Jake, can I blindfold you and kiss you all over?"

His green eyes twinkled. "Hell yeah."

She darted to her suitcase, hunted for a bikini wrap that when folded over would double nicely as a blindfold, and then turned around to find he'd already shed his shorts and T-shirt. Her skin heated up at the sight of his broad, toned body, his firm muscles and tanned skin.

"Bed. Now," she said, and he stretched out.

She climbed over him and tied the wrap over his eyes, then raked her eyes over him from head to toe. Sparks shot through her as she took him in on the bed, clad only in boxer briefs. He looked hot like that, his strong chest and sturdy arms on display and the rigid lines between his abs self-evident. Not to mention the fact that the white boxers left little to the imagination about his desire for her.

"Give me thirty seconds to put on some music and slip into something more comfortable," she said, then grabbed her phone and called up a Jane Black song. Once the music started, she quietly picked up his shorts from the floor, snagged his wallet, and opened it, flipping through it quickly. Diamonds were small. If he had found diamonds in Isla's office, he could have hidden them in his wallet and claimed he'd uncovered none.

But the leather fold contained only credit cards and greenbacks.

Next, she dipped her hand into the back pocket of his shorts, checking there, too, as the clock ticked. Her heart beat furiously, pounding in her ears, as he lay calmly on the bed. Happily waiting for her as she raced through his clothes.

"Tick tock, Steph. You should be about naked now or wearing the red lacy thong I'm picturing you in," he said in a playful tone, parking his hands behind his head.

So trusting. So happy to be here.

Her shoulders tensed. "Almost there," she said from her spot kneeling on the floor as she reached into the front pocket and wrapped her hands around a . . . jar of honey?

She took it out, and then burst into a wide smile. He had a jar of the honey she loved. That was too cute. Too adorable. And she was too confused.

Something just didn't add up.

Something made no sense at all.

All the evidence pointed to Jake Harlowe telling the truth about today's visit to the gallery—that he'd come up empty-handed.

If he had, that meant he wasn't hiding any of Isla's diamonds from Steph.

She also knew he hadn't pilfered Isla's stone last night. He had an alibi—Steph herself.

That also meant someone else took her stone.

That was bad.

She dragged a hand through her hair, then shrugged. Fuck it. Time to come clean with the hot, sexy man in her bed. But as she dropped one knee to the bed and crawled over to him, she sat up straight.

A loud rapping echoed in the room.

Someone was knocking on the door.

Several times. Over and over.

"This is the hotel manager."

Shit.

In seconds, Jake had untied his blindfold.

"I'd better answer that," she said, and Jake scrambled to pull on his shorts while she headed to the door.

She opened it to find a tall, red-haired man with a mustache. He was dressed in gray slacks, a white shirt, a tie, and a suit jacket. A brass name tag on the jacket revealed his name: ALFREDO.

He bowed his head slightly. "Hello, Ms. Anderson," he said in a friendly but apologetic voice. "So sorry to disturb you this afternoon, but I wanted to check and make sure you had received the paperwork for your meeting."

She knit her eyebrows together. A small kernel of worry took hold inside her. "I'm sorry, but what meeting are you referring to?"

"The meeting you had this morning, I believe?"

Jake walked over to the door, joined her in the entryway, and draped an arm across her waist. The gesture felt strangely comforting, and she both wanted it and was sure she didn't deserve it. Not after doubting him the way she had.

"I didn't have a meeting today," she said to the hotel manager, tilting her head to the side. "And I didn't receive any paperwork."

"Oh dear," the manager said, scratching his chin.

"Which means I have no clue what you're talking about. Care to enlighten me?"

The manager pressed his hands together, steepling his fingers as if in prayer. "Yesterday evening, around six o'clock p.m., a man came to the front desk and said you had a meeting with him today. He informed us he needed to drop off some paperwork in advance. He asked if he could bring it to your room, but of course we said no."

The hair on her neck stood on end.

Jake flinched. "Good. No one needs to be in her room," he said, his tone thoroughly protective.

"Absolutely. We do not give out our guests' information. That's why my clerk took the envelope and brought it to your room himself. He marked in the delivery log that he left it here yesterday evening, around six fifteen. He left it on the desk in the room, and I came by to make sure you had received it." He paused and gestured to the desk, bereft of envelopes. "But it seems you don't have it."

Steph gulped and shook her head, nerves swimming wildly through her now. "No. I don't have it. But maybe I missed it," she said. She scanned the desk and the bureau, but there were no envelopes or papers. She returned her gaze to the manager. "There's nothing here."

The carrot-topped man nodded and sighed. "Let me check with the clerk to double confirm it was delivered."

"Wait," Steph said. "Who was the man dropping off the papers? What was his name?"

"Mr. Smith, I believe," the manager said, then swiveled around and marched down the hallway. Steph watched him go, her heart beating out a staccato rhythm of fear and worry. Could the clerk have stolen her diamond when he delivered the papers to her room? But if he had, why would the paperwork have disappeared, too? Someone, it seemed, had tried to trick the hotel into giving up her room number by faking a meeting with her and using a fake name.

Because Mr. Smith was as phony a name as there ever was.

Who the hell was Mr. Smith?

She shut the door and turned to Jake, her world spinning like a mad teacup ride in an amusement park.

She swayed, and the floor felt wobbly. "I think someone pretended he had a meeting with me, followed the clerk as he delivered the paperwork for the fake meeting, then broke into my room later in the night," she said in a tiny whisper.

His jaw dropped, and his eyes widened. "Why? When?" He pointed in the direction of the hotel manager. "Because of what the manager just said?"

"Yes," she said, and her voice croaked.

He tilted his head, looked at her like he was studying her. "So this 'Mr. Smith' claimed a meeting as a ruse to get in your room?" he asked, sketching air quotes around the name.

Her stomach plummeted with nerves. "Look around. There are no papers in here, and I have no clue what's going on. But someone must have broken in—"

"Wait. Is that why you were patting me down earlier?" He crossed his arms. "You dragged me from the gallery, and you treated me like you didn't trust me. Did you think I took something from your room?"

"I was worried it was you," she spat out, the words tumbling free before she could even think twice about what she was saying. Before she could even analyze the risk in admitting that she didn't trust a damn soul right now. She squeezed her eyes shut. When she opened them, a tear slipped down her face. She wiped her hand across her cheek. "I freaked out, because I trusted you. I let you into my room and my body, and this morning after I showered, the diamond was gone. Completely gone."

He stumbled backward, his arm shot out, and he grabbed the wall. "Are you serious?" he whispered. "From your safe?"

She nodded. "I thought it was you. Because I found it missing right after you left. Jake, what else would I think?"

He shot her a look like she was crazy. "*Anything*. Anything but that."

"But you know how to break into safes. You broke into mine before."

He held out his hands wide and shook his head. Anger seemed to roll off him like smoke. "I would *never* steal from you."

"But you figured out the combo before. In seconds."

"And you changed it, right?"

She nodded. "Yes, but I thought maybe you figured it out again."

He huffed and inhaled deeply, then dragged a hand roughly through his hair. He paced to the window, then back again. "Please tell me you didn't change it back to *A-R-I-E-L*."

"No, it was—"

He cut her off. "I don't want to know what it is." He sighed in frustration, then fixed her with a stare. "Why are you telling me this now if you thought I stole the diamond?"

Time to 'fess up. To tell all. "Because Isla told me this afternoon that the diamond in her necklace was stolen last night, too. And with this Mr. Smith dropping off fake papers and with you not having any diamonds in your wallet—"

He blinked. "Diamonds in my wallet?"

"I blindfolded you," she said, lowering her eyes, guilt stitched into her voice. As she breathed the words aloud, she realized how silly they sounded. She'd tricked the man she slept with to learn if he'd tricked her. "To see if you hid diamonds from Isla's gallery in your wallet," she admitted, letting her confession free in one quick breath.

His eyes widened. He shook his head several times, as if he could barely conceive of her deception. "You went through my wallet? While I was blindfolded and waiting for you to get undressed? Even though I told you there were no diamonds in her gallery?"

"Well, you did give me your wallet a few days ago to hold on to as collateral," she said, pointing out that little detail. As if that were her free pass to riffle through it.

"I know. But Steph." His voice rose. "What the hell? I trusted you."

Trust. It was practically a four-letter word. It was what she longed for. It was what she'd tried to believe in. But if she didn't entirely trust her own stepfather, how could she trust anyone else, especially a man gunning for him?

"And I trusted you," she said, placing her palms together, imploring him. "I did. I swear I did. I woke up this morning having had the most amazing time with you last night and feeling like we were on the same page. Then my diamond went missing. All I could think was you took it. What else was I supposed to think?"

"You weren't supposed to think. You were supposed to talk. To me. About it. Because I didn't do it," he said softly, his green eyes locking onto hers.

"I believe that now."

"Then let's figure out who might have done it. Tell me what happened."

CHAPTER SEVEN

She took his hand and led him to the safe. She opened it and gestured inside, recounting every detail of her morning.

". . . And then I noticed a sliver of light by the door. When I pulled on the door after the shower, the safe was completely empty and the diamond was gone. I don't even care about the diamond for me. I wasn't going to keep it. That diamond was my one small bit of insurance that I could still have something for my mom as a way to pay her back for how she helped me. But if it's part of the stolen stash, I'd obviously return it to Andrew and the fund."

Jake pointed to his chest, annoyance still thick in his veins. "But you thought I took it?"

She shrugged, a guilty look in her pretty blue eyes. "You already showed me you knew how to take it," she said in a small but certain voice. "You were in my room all night. You were in my room alone when I talked to the room service guy."

Her voice quivered, and he could tell she felt so damn guilty. Still, he was ticked that she'd made this assumption. "I'm not that guy," he said firmly.

"I know that now," she said, wringing her hands, a tear sliding down her cheek. "But I didn't know what to think then."

That errant tear did him in. It revealed her fears, and he longed to erase them. To carry them himself. He wrapped his arms around her and tugged her close. He was pissed that she thought he'd taken her diamond, but he also completely understood her reaction. To get out of the shower and find something precious stolen when you'd slept with a man who cracked safes was like opening the door and inviting in the perpetrator.

He knew the truth, though. He hadn't taken the gem.

Someone else had, though, and that fact changed everything. Doubt or no doubt, trust or lack thereof, all that mattered to Jake was her safety.

"You can't stay here any longer," he said in a firm voice as they stood by the foot of the bed. "It's not safe. Someone else is after the diamonds, too."

She lowered her voice and whispered, "Do you think they sneaked in before we were here last night or while we were sleeping?"

"I think they were here when we were on the boat. Not while I was here. I would have heard it."

"Oh really? Do you have supersonic hearing?" she asked, parking her hands on her hips. The air-conditioning whirred in the room as he shot her a stare.

"No, Miss Sarcastic. But I'm pretty sure I'd have noticed someone slipping into the room and opening a safe even if I was deep in the Land of Nod. Besides, if it were me taking something, I'd do it when no one was around."

She arched an eyebrow. "See?"

"See what? You still think I did it? Because I have an opinion on how it was pulled off?"

She sliced a hand through the air. "Forget I said that. I just want to move on. Because . . . Jake," she said softly, her voice wobbly, etched with frustration. "This is not what I wanted when I came to the Caymans. I just wanted to do my tour, and help my mom, and talk to Eli. And now someone is breaking into my room to steal diamonds, and maybe it's the same person who took Isla's, too."

"No way are these just two coincidental burglaries of the same watermarked stones on the same night. This is a case of someone in hot pursuit of all the diamonds, too. Who the hell is this Mr. Smith? That's what I want to know," he said, then a memory of a car blasted front and center in his mind. He stopped in his tracks. "Shit. The green Honda." He resumed his pace around the room, quickly explaining the car he'd seen earlier in the week that he thought was following Eli. He'd seen it again today when conducting recon at the church window. "Tall guy. Gray hair. Know anyone who fits that description?"

She arched an eyebrow. "That's kind of broad. I mean, if we're looking for a tall guy with gray hair, we might as well be looking for anyone. Can we narrow that down at all?"

"I don't have gray hair," he said with a mischievous glint. "But the way we narrow it down is to figure out who else knows that Eli has a stash of diamonds." He paused. "Penny knew."

"It wasn't Penny. She's a little—"

"Flighty?"

"Yeah."

"So who knows Eli has one thousand diamonds? Well, minus two," he said, stopping to meet her eyes. "You know he has them now? We're not going back to that whole *what-if-he-didn't-take-the-diamonds* line, are we?"

Her jaw seemed to tighten, but she managed a crisp nod. "I will acknowledge he has diamonds. I'm not Cleopatra, Queen of Denial."

"Good. Because it looks like we might have competition in finding them. To figure out who is after the diamonds, we need to figure out who knows about them and why this person would steal from Eli. And unfortunately, Mr. Smith seems to be after not only *the* diamonds, but also onto *you*. This person knew you had a diamond, a very expensive diamond. I'll say it again—you're not safe here. So I don't give a crap if you trust me or not. You're going to stay with me."

She eyed him quizzically, staring at him on the other side of her hotel bed, the same bed they'd broken in last night and again this morning, the same one where she'd been ready to frisk him. "With you? In your room? Like we're lovers on a vacation?"

He laughed, and the sound turned into a scoff. "You can have your own separate bed, Ma," he said, affecting an old man's voice. "Would that make you feel better?"

She answered by rolling her eyes. Despite the tension that ran thick between them, he got a kick out of ribbing her still. "Thanks, Pa. Hope you enjoy your twin bed, too, for your old aches and pains."

"I will. And I won't let some hot, young, whippersnapper foxy lady stay someplace that got robbed." He dropped the teasing tone and locked eyes with her. "No matter how you slice it, someone was in your room last night and took a ten-thousand-dollar jewel. I want you by my side. I will keep you safe. I'm good at it. It's what I do."

The rough edges around her melted away, and she smiled sweetly. "Thank you for saying that. Especially since I know you're still mad at me over my terrible blindfolding skills."

"They were pretty bad," he said, then walked around the bed and dropped a hand to her shoulder. "Say you'll stay with me."

"I'm leaving for a tour in three days."

"Then that gives us seventy-two hours to figure this out."

Her lips quirked up. "What if Mr. Smith is onto *us*? Is it bad if we're seen together?"

"My gut tells me Mr. Smith is angling for Eli, and that's why diamonds that Eli gave his fiancée and his stepdaughter were stolen. Someone is after the diamonds, and that someone knows you had one and Isla had one. We just need to keep being stealthy, but we've always had to be stealthy. Now, we need to work together to stay ahead of Mr. Smith."

She stepped closer. "It really wasn't you who did it?"

He moved in closer, his chest to hers, breathing in her sexy scent. Minutes ago, he'd been ready for her to run her hands all over him. He'd wanted it. He still did. That was the rub. "It wasn't me. Because if it were me, I wouldn't be back. If I were stealing your diamond, I wouldn't be here with you now. I wouldn't invite you to my room. I wouldn't need you to solve this case. I'd leave. I'd walk away from you and I'd get the hell out of town with a bird in the hand. But I like you, even though I'm mad at you, and that's why I want you to stay with me. This isn't just about us finding diamonds. It's about us making sure those fingers don't get pointed at us. So let's solve this bitch of a case together."

He held out a hand to seal the deal.

She took it and shook. "This is the craziest trip ever to the Cayman Islands."

"I agree." He dipped a hand into his shorts pocket. "Oh, I did steal something." He took the small honey jar from his pocket. "I saw it on a room service tray on my way out this morning and I grabbed it to give to you. As a silly little gift, since you love the hotel's weirdly amazing honey. I'm pretty sure you felt it when you were patting me down."

"I did."

"What did you think it was?"

"Well, I didn't think it was *that*!"

He laughed. "Now we're getting somewhere. But you did think it was the jewels for a minute, right?" he asked, eyeing her with a *c'mon-admit-it* stare.

She shrugged her admission.

"Let's put it this way," she said, wrapping her hands around his fingers on the jar. "I'm glad to know the jar doesn't have honey-coated diamonds in it."

CHAPTER EIGHT

He dropped her suitcase on the tiled floor. A fan circled lazily overhead, stirring the gauzy white curtains that hung by the sliding glass doors. He grabbed her hand, pulled her to the open deck. The sun was still high in the sky and his room had a stunning view of the endless blue water. He also had a clear view of how to resolve this turmoil still roiling in his chest.

On the one hand, he was grateful she came with him to his hotel, and he was thrilled to see her out of harm's way. On the other hand, he wanted her to know the truth of who he was. No more lies. No more doubts. They'd had it out, for all intents and purposes, in her room, as the rush of anger coupled with the urgent need to get her safe ruled the moment. Now, it was time to let go of the defensiveness and try to understand each other. If they were working together—and hell, that sure seemed to be the plan—they had to be on the same side.

Otherwise, he'd walk away. But the thought of leaving her made his gut clench.

He had to try to talk to her about some of the harder topics. If not, this would be Rosalinda and the Medici job all over again.

"Just look," he said, gesturing to the vast sea.

She gazed toward the water. "It's gorgeous."

"It is. And I'm showing you to make a point."

"Over the view?" She parked her hands on the railing.

He turned to her and met her eyes. "Yes. I'm showing you this because it's beautiful. Because you love the water. Because you are an outdoor girl through and through. Because I know these things about you," he said, taking her hands and clasping them in his. He squeezed. "I know already that the water calms you. I know the sunshine is like some kind of magic to you. And I know you love your mother with a fierceness that can move mountains. You're like this warrior princess who'd go to battle for her, and even though I've never met her, I can picture her. I imagine she is the gentlest, kindest person in the world who wouldn't hurt a fly, and you fight for her. Not because she's the kind of woman who won't fight for herself, but rather because she chooses not to. Am I right?"

Steph drew in a deep breath and nodded. A warm breeze blew by, stirring up the ends of her pretty blonde hair. "Yes. You're right." Her voice was soft.

As the waves lapped the shore in the distance, and boaters skipped over the blue waters, he grasped her arms. "But what do you know about me?"

She opened her lips but didn't speak.

"Steph," he said, fixing her with a sharp gaze, and then asked again, needing to set her straight, desperate to avoid another on-the-job mistake. "What do you know about me?"

"That you like ice cream?" She said it like a question, her expression confused.

He nodded, a sliver of a smile appearing briefly. "That's a good start. What else?"

"That you like to tell jokes?" she asked, squinting as the sun shone brightly overhead.

"Keep going."

"That you're motivated by your family," she said with more confidence now in her tone.

"Good. Keep going."

"That you do what you do because of them. To take care of your little sister and brother, and your big sister's kid."

"I do."

"And that you hate when bastards get away with anything."

He tapped his finger to his nose. *Bingo.* "Know what else?"

"What?"

A knot of discomfort clogged his throat. He pushed past it, speaking plainly, honestly. "I went out with a woman who nearly cost me a job. Who tried to steal the artifact we'd teamed up to find," he said, the memory blasting through him of how foolish he'd felt when Rosalinda stole it from him. "I trusted her. I thought she cared about me. She only cared about the prize."

"I don't even want the prize," Steph said, raising her chin, meeting his gaze. "I'm not after money. I'm after the truth."

"But it seemed this morning that you were playing me," he said, his tone turning rougher. "That when you saw me at the café, you were all sexy snuggly because you thought I'd run. And outside the gallery, you were pretending to get cozy when you put your hands in my shorts, but you were only searching for stones even after I told you there weren't any."

"I was," she said through gritted teeth. Her expression was one of frustration and embarrassment.

"Don't fuck with my feelings. You know I want you. You know I like you. Just don't fuck with me," he said, yanking her close to him.

"I'm not. I won't. I'm sorry," she said, her tone full of contrition.

That knot unwound, and he nodded. "So tell me the truth. Do I seem like the type of guy who'd screw you over?"

She sighed, but smiled softly. "No. You don't seem like that kind of guy."

He raised a hand and brushed the back of his fingertips against her cheek. Her skin was so soft. She smelled so good. "You tell me what kind of guy you think I am."

She leaned into his hand on her cheek. "A good guy," she whispered, her voice breathy as her eyes never strayed from his.

He nodded, glad that she'd said it. That he hadn't put those words in her mouth. "I am. I am a good guy," he repeated.

"You are. You really are," she said, angling her hips, her body seeking out contact. He tugged her against him so the only thing she felt was how damn hard he was.

This woman drove him wild. She was a pistol, a fiery, sexy, determined, tenacious woman who made him crazy, and who he wanted fiercely at the same damn time. "Do you want to try that whole thing again? Like you were doing in your room. Take off my shirt, and strip off my shorts, and pull off my boxers?"

Her lips quirked up. "I didn't get to the boxers."

"I know," he said, raising an eyebrow. "Damn shame. Because I like it when you touch me. I like it when you take my clothes off and run your hands all over me. Do you like it when I do that to you?"

She nodded. "So much. So incredibly much," she said, her voice breathy.

He backed her up against the railing, pressing his pelvis to her and caging her in with his arms. "Are you sure?"

He ground his hips against her, letting her feel the full length of his arousal.

Her breath came fast. "So sure," she said, wrapping her arms around his lower back and tugging him close. "I want to finish what we were starting in the room."

He laughed loudly and deeply. "Oh Steph. We barely got started. We hardly got started at all."

She grabbed his shirt. "Can we please just fuck it out now?"

He cracked up at her question, at the sexy desperation in her voice. "Fuck it out?"

She nodded. "Yes. Your anger. Our mistrust. My doubt. Can we just once and for all fuck it out and let it go?"

He clasped her cheeks in his hands. "I can't think of a damn thing I'd rather do now than fuck it out. Besides, it's impossible for me to think straight and properly plan the next phase of Project Diamond unless you put your hands on the railing, bend over, and raise your skirt for me."

Her eyes lit up, sparkling with a naughty kind of excitement. "Then please allow me to help you think straight."

He laced a hand through her hair, yanked her close, and planted a hot, searing kiss on her delicious lips. She melted under his touch, and he loved it. Loved the way she responded.

As he kissed her, he lowered a hand to her leg and inched his fingers up the warm skin of her thighs, quickly finding what he wanted—the wet scrap of fabric between her legs. She was so damn turned on, just like he was. He groaned as he kissed her, his bones vibrating with lust as he ran his fingers against the evidence of her desire. He tugged off her underwear, broke the kiss, and spun her around.

Covering her back with his chest, he wrapped her hair in his hand and tugged gently. She gasped and arched her ass higher. Yup. That was his answer. She liked a little rough play. He brought his mouth to her ear. "Do you like it hard? Do you like it rough? Do you like it angry?"

She turned her head to look at him. "With you, so far I like everything."

He grasped her chin and held her gaze, staring at her. "Good. Stay here."

He headed inside, grabbed a condom, and returned to the gorgeous sight on his balcony—Steph, with her sundress bunched up above her hips, her panties on the ground, and her lovely, delicious body ready for him.

"Take off your shirt," she said, her voice all dreamy sexy.

He grabbed the hem and yanked it off. "Why did you want it off?" he asked playfully.

"Because you're hot. I like looking at you."

"But you're going to be looking at the ocean."

"I like feeling you, then. That OK?"

He unzipped his shorts, let them fall to the floor, and stepped out of them. "You like feeling me. Hmm. Why's that?"

"Because your body is insane, and I love the way it fits me."

"It?" he asked, with an arch of the brow as he tugged off his briefs. "It?"

"It. You. Your body. You're so hot. Looking at you turns me on," she said, her eyes on him as he rolled on the condom. He was so damn ready. Needed this so badly. He'd wanted her since this morning. Mostly, he wanted to get rid of all the frustration stemming from their cat-and-mouse games. No better way than the physical. It was the one thing that didn't lie. It was a language comprised only of truth. There was no doubt to the way she glistened for him. To how hot she was. To the lift in her hips, the look in her eyes, the rise and fall of her chest as she breathed hard.

There was nothing but truth to the way he ached to fill her.

He positioned himself at her slick entrance, and in one delicious thrust, he pushed inside her. All the way. They moaned in unison. He snaked an arm around her chest, sliding his hand between her breasts and up to her neck. Then he pumped.

Like that, with a rough, hard rhythm, he showed her the truth.

"This, Steph. This isn't a lie," he said in a growl, in her ear.

"I know," she said, gasping as he drove into her.

"This is the truth. The way we fit like this."

"I know. Oh God, I know," she said, her voice rising as he moved in her.

It was the purity of the connection. It was what brought them together in the first place. Here and now, on this balcony, overlooking the Atlantic Ocean, with all the tourists below who had no clue diamonds were being stolen across the land, and hearts were being toyed with, and heists were plotted and replotted, he proved the one thing he could.

That this connection between them was real. It was honest.

It might not last. It might have an expiration date. But for now, as he thrust into her, this was as true as the sun blazing overhead. It was as real as the waves crashing onto the shore.

She rose up on her toes, bowed her back, and gripped the railing. He brought his hands to her hips, dug his thumbs into her bones, and took her hard. She panted, and moaned, and cried his name. Soon her cries were coming faster, and he was sure someone else in the hotel might hear, but there was no way he could care. Not as she clenched around him, rocked her hips, and whispered that she was coming.

She shuddered several times as he drove into her. He followed her there, his own orgasm tearing through him, blasting into every corner of his body. He found his release as pleasure whipped through his body, and the world winked on and off as he came.

Then he grabbed her hair and tugged it.

She yelped, a playful, satisfied sound.

"I guess you like having your hair pulled," he growled in her ear.

"I do," she said as he pulled out of her.

He disposed of the condom, then scooped her into his lap on a deck chair, and he held her. "I'm sorry someone broke into your room," he said softly, then kissed her cheek.

"Me, too."

"You're safe with me. Know that, Steph. Just know that."

"I do know that. And I do know you, and I like you."

"Same here," he said, then wrapped his arms around her.

He liked this contact, too, far too much for his own good.

CHAPTER NINE

They showered, and he washed her hair, then soaped her body. She savored every second of it as he moved his hands from her breasts, to her belly, down her legs. She was slippery and wet, and he couldn't take his hands off her.

She liked it that way. She loved the attention. She was damn glad they'd moved past her doubts over him. Sure, she might be facing a whole new spate of them when it came to the case, but she was facing them head-on with him—a partner and a temporary lover. He excelled at both roles, she was learning.

"I'm hardly dirty," she said as he spent more time than needed washing her calves.

"I know, but I can't seem to stop touching you. Your fault for being so sexy," he said, then he stood and dropped a kiss on her nose. She smiled and sighed happily.

She wasn't wild about fighting, but a misunderstanding that led to hard, hot make-up sex and a tender moment in the shower was A-OK in her book. She grabbed the bar of soap and returned the shower favor, washing his arms, flat belly, and back. She shampooed his hair, too, loving the way the wet strands felt in her hands. She leaned his head back under the spray and rinsed the shampoo. Soon, they stepped out of the shower and toweled off.

Her stomach growled.

He arched an eyebrow in question.

"I think I'm hungry. I haven't eaten since we had eggs for breakfast many moons ago. Want to take me on a date, roomie?" she asked with a coquettish jut of her shoulder, as if she were reeling him back in.

He shook his head, bemused as he finger-combed his hair. "You crack me up. You go from thinking I stole from you to wanting me to take you out for food?"

"I do," she said, wiggling her eyebrows as she met his gaze in the mirror.

"Then I'm taking you on a date. Even though you're a pain in the ass, but evidently that's one of the things I like most about you. So get ready to be wined and dined," he said, giving her an order.

She clicked her bare heels together and saluted. "Yes sir. May I have the lotion now? And a full report on your findings from the gallery, sir?"

"I've only been trying to tell you about it since I left, but you had your mind on other things." He handed her the hotel lotion.

"I did, but now you've satisfied me, so I'm ready," she said, even though she knew sex wasn't what he'd meant.

As she rubbed lotion into her legs, he explained what he'd found at the gallery. "Here's what happened. As soon as I got into Isla's office, I knew Penny's tip was wrong about the diamonds. I'm not saying she lied or anything. Just that whatever knowledge she had no longer applied. There were clearly no gems in Isla's office at all."

"I think she worked there a while ago, so maybe her info was out of date," she offered.

He squirted toothpaste onto a brush. "Yeah, that's probably what happened. Because the walls were completely bare. Not a damn thing on them. But, being the brilliant private-eye-slash-bounty-hunter that I am," he said, tapping his temple, "I wasn't going to squander my chance and cry in the chicken soup over the absence of frames. I did some digging."

"Naturally."

"Looked through some drawers. Pawed around the desk. Made sure she wasn't hiding the diamonds elsewhere. And fortunately, Isla is quite organized. Did you know that?" he asked, then began to brush his teeth.

"No. I haven't been debriefed on her organizational skills. Please, do share all you know about how she sorts her drawers."

He smirked, brushed, and spat out the toothpaste. "She's a dream to investigate. She has nothing. Her office is like a shrine to simplicity. I think she's one of those people who hates things."

"Except for sex toys and olives."

"Well, obviously. Sex toys are awesome, and olives aren't so bad. In any case, she has one of those sleek metal desks with one drawer. Only pens in it and a Moleskine notebook. She had some nuts on her desk."

"Nuts?" She arched an eyebrow.

"They usually grow on trees, they're high in protein and fat, and you eat them. You're familiar with nuts?"

She tapped her chin as if deep in thought. "Ah, yes. Nuts. Now I understand." She rolled her eyes. "Point being, that's an unusual thing to have on your desk."

"Maybe she keeps nuts around for a quick protein hit. Anyway, she also has only one file cabinet. And it's not even the metal kind. It's one of those fancy, cloth-drawer thingamajiggers that women like."

"We all like fancy cloth file cabinet drawers?"

"Oh, I'm sorry. Was that an overgeneralization?" he asked drily.

She held her thumb and forefinger together.

"Anyway, so on the top of it I found some paperwork and that's what I took. Basically, it's a document saying Isla donated fifty grand last month to a charity that builds schools in Africa. It's in one of the countries where there was a ton of diamond mining with child labor, and kids were affected by it. This charity was set up to help them go to school and earn an education."

"Is it the one where she's listed on the website as being a major donor?" she asked, then gave him the name of the charity.

He nodded. "Same one."

She dropped her towel and enjoyed the way his eyes followed her naked body even as she left the bathroom and headed to her suitcase. "Do you think she's cashing in diamonds for charity? You said before you thought they might be converting some of the diamonds bit by bit," Steph asked from the room, focusing on the notion of Isla *and* Eli, not just Eli pulling off this con solo.

"That would be an interesting twist, wouldn't it?" Jake said as she pulled on panties and a bra, then hunted for her blue dress with slim white stripes. "First night I was here, I saw at her gallery that the Lynx paintings sold for five thousand a piece. Today, when I peeked in the drawer in her gallery, the records show that she'd sold ten of them."

"Maybe she's putting the proceeds from her gallery into this charity. Do you think it's connected?" Steph asked as she shrugged on the light cotton dress.

Jake emerged from the bathroom, and it was her turn to enjoy an eyeful of his naked glory, and my, was he glorious. She frowned as he put on boxers. "Makes me sad to see you in clothes."

"Speaking of clothes, you need to add a bikini," he said, gesturing to her dress.

She lifted an eyebrow. "Something you want to tell me?"

He fixed her with a stare. "Yes. That *something* is bring a bikini for tonight."

She smiled, grabbed one, and stuffed it into her purse. "Done."

"Excellent. And to answer your question, there seems to be some kind of connection. There has to be," he said as he grabbed a pair of cargo shorts.

She clasped her hand over her mouth as an idea slammed into her. "What if they cashed out all the diamonds, Jake? What if there is no more missing money? Maybe it's a lost cause," she whispered, frowning, as the possibility of coming up empty-handed clanged in her brain. No justice, no chance to do the right thing. What if the thieves got away with it?

"It happens," he said in a matter-of-fact tone as he snagged a shirt from the closet and put it on. "Not every job is solvable. Sometimes people move on and the money is gone, even when there's proof, like there is here. We don't know what they've done with the diamonds they bought from the Frayer mine. All we know for sure is a few were stolen, and they're supporting a charity for those affected by the diamond economy," he said.

"And what if we find them? You're not going to turn him in, are you?"

Jake shook his head. "I work for clients. My client wants this handled as quietly as possible."

"Will Andrew turn him in?" she asked, quaking with worry.

"I don't have that answer, but he seems more focused on restoring the money than on turning him in."

That's why it was even more important for her to get to the diamonds before the thieves did. Besides, if the diamonds went back to Andrew's company, that wasn't a bad option, either. They certainly didn't seem to belong to Eli, and the thought that her stepdad might be a thief was like an injection of pure sadness in her bloodstream.

"I need to see him again," she said, swallowing thickly, fighting back the kernel of worry camped out in her. This was the hard part. Confronting him. But if she was ever going to get to the bottom of this, she had to stay ahead of the others who were after his stones. She had to use her advantages. "I'll give him a call in a few minutes. Set something up. See what I can find out."

"Maybe another breakfast at Tristan's."

That name jogged her memory. Tristan. Tall. Gray-haired. *"Tristan."*

He nodded. "Right, the guy who owns the restaurant."

"Yes," she said quickly. "But he's also tall and has gray hair."

Jake's eyes widened. "Go on. Does he own a green Honda?"

"That I don't know. But what if he's going after the diamonds? He works near the bank, and remember that time I saw him on the diamond merchant street when I grabbed you and made out with you so he wouldn't see me?"

"I could never forget a prelude to the first time you came screaming my name."

She rolled her eyes.

"Don't roll your eyes. It's true. You came hard in the back of the car and you were absolutely calling my name."

"Fine. Yes, it was epic. But back to Tristan. Could he be after them? Do you think he's our Mr. Smith?"

"It's possible," he said. "What's his motivation, though? Usually, there's a specific one."

She snapped her fingers. "Eli said Tristan wanted to do business with him, but he didn't seem too interested. Maybe Tristan is pissed because Eli turned down a business deal?"

"Nice work, Sherlock. Let's make him suspect number one."

She nearly jumped in place when another idea slammed into her. "Wait. There wasn't any art in the gallery office, right?"

"Correct."

"But Penny said Eli was always checking out the frames in the gallery office," she said, making a rolling gesture with her fingers as the words spilled out of her lips, coming as quickly as the clues added up. "And Isla told me as I was leaving today that they moved the diamonds. And if the walls are bare in her office, but there's art hanging in the nightclub in oddly shaped frames . . ." She knit her eyebrows, letting him reach the same conclusion.

"You think they're in the frames at Sapphire?"

She nodded, and a wide smile spread across her face. "I think Isla and Eli have some weird obsession with that art and that artist, and it's because they think they found the perfect hiding place for their jewels. Inside the frames of his art."

He quirked up one corner of his lips and shook his head. "I doubt he'd put diamonds in artwork in the hallway."

"No, but didn't you say he had some art on the walls in his office the night you scoped it out? But his manager walked out of the office so you couldn't check it out?"

He stroked his chin and nodded approvingly. "I'm beginning to think we need to plan a return visit to Sapphire."

"Yes," she said as she adjusted the straps on her dress. "Perhaps we can get to the bottom of this Sapphire affair."

∽ꝍ∽

As Steph called her stepdad and finished doing those things women do before dates, Jake wandered along the stone path that edged the hotel property. Time to update his client, and it was best to have this call out of earshot of other guests.

"This case is getting crazier, Andrew," he said into the phone, his flip-flops slapping across the cobbled path on the way to the beach. "I've got to hand it to the guy. Eli knows how to hide things."

Andrew heaved a sigh, but then tried to remain chipper. "But all the evidence points in the right direction. He did turn the stolen money to diamonds via the merchant, and it's in the Caymans. So we can't be too far off."

Jake laughed and scoffed at the same time at his client's optimistic attitude. It wasn't that simple. Good jobs never were. "On the surface, yes. But I honestly don't know if we're going to get the diamonds because I don't know if he still has them," he said, slowing his pace as he rubbed a hand against the back of his neck.

Andrew grumbled something that sounded like a string of curse words.

"Sorry, but it happens," Jake said.

"I know, but I want to do everything I can to find the diamonds and return them to the fund. We have the proof, and if we can get them back, we can restore the fund more quickly than if we have to go through lengthy legal battles. I want to do it before we have to go to the SEC and make this more public. I've got customers talking about pulling out their money. Others are stressing about what was lost. I need to do everything I can before this gets out and our fund starts to go under."

"I hear ya," Jake said, but he highly doubted Eli would be moved by any sort of confrontation. The man was impervious. "And don't think for a second that I'm throwing in the towel. Just want you to know the score." Jake stopped to lean against a palm tree, staring out at the water. "We've narrowed it down from art to jewels, and we've got a few leads, but now some of the diamonds are being stolen. We've got someone else after them, since one of the diamonds was taken from Steph and one from Eli's fiancée."

"Steph's still involved?"

"We ran into each other and figured out we were after the same thing. So we're teaming up on this one," he said, resuming his pace along the path, keeping the Steph details simple. No need for Andrew to know they were sharing both a room and orgasms.

"She's a lovely lady. She got her good looks from her mother."

Jake startled at the odd remark. "Not sure what that has to do with anything, but be that as it may, we're working on this, and, evidently, so are others. I'll go the distance, but I need to know if that's what you want."

"Do what you can do. My shareholders are breathing down my neck. But please don't commit any crimes to get there," Andrew said, nerves pocked in his voice.

"Like breaking and entering? That sort of thing?" Jake asked wryly.

"Exactly."

"I'll do my best to stay above the law."

Andrew cleared his throat, and Jake expected him to say good-bye. "Listen, I'll offer you a bonus if you can pull this off," he said, then rattled off a healthy number.

Jake blinked and stopped in his tracks. That would cover a lot of summer school. It would pay down a big chunk of law school. It would make life a hell of a lot easier. All he'd have to do would be to beat the competition and do it before Steph left for her tour in three days.

"You're on," he said, and returned to his room and his date. The next few hours were a reprieve from the hunt for jewels, and he intended to enjoy them to the fullest.

And her.

CHAPTER TEN

Later that evening, Jake glided across the sandy bottom of the seafloor at Eden Rock, sweeping a flashlight along the caves by the sand gully, drinking in oxygen from the regulator. The grottos underwater made for a perfect dive at dusk. As they explored a craggy cave, a school of silvery grassy sweepers darted past, stirring the cool waters forty feet below the surface.

Jake had gone on many dives in Key Largo, since his hometown was one of the top scuba destinations in the world. But Steph was the pro here, and her ease in the water was evident as she slipped through the rocky tunnels. He hadn't told her in advance this was on the agenda for their hastily planned date, just to bring a bikini. That surprise factor worked, and it made her delight when they arrived at Eden Rock Dive Shop an hour ago all the more fun to witness. She'd bounced on her toes when she found out what they were doing—a thirty-minute sunset dive.

The site was so close to shore that they'd walked into the water, then swum one hundred and fifty yards to the buoy that marked Eden Rock.

A tarpon slipped past, nearly smacking him with a fin. Sea plants swayed in the ocean. But with air running low, it was time to say good-bye to the ocean. They rose up. As they broke the glassy surface, shades of vibrant pink and bright orange streaked across the sky. The sun raced toward the edge of the earth, flaring its final rays of the day in a radiant sunset.

They treaded water and watched the brilliant orb descend below the horizon in a burst of colors, then a glorious fade to dusk. He shifted his gaze to his date. He said nothing because words weren't needed. The natural beauty said it all and so did her eyes—they sparkled as she stared into the distance. This was her happy place and he was lucky to share it with her.

Fifteen minutes later, they emerged from the water and reached the dive shop. He returned their equipment and they headed to his rental car. The air-conditioning in her Jeep had been on the fritz, so they'd driven in his car.

"Thank you for taking me on a dive. It was perfection," she said as he opened the passenger door for her.

"You're welcome, but I'm pretty sure you were the one taking me," he corrected. "You're the pro. I'm just along for the ride. I will, however, finally take you to dinner. Seemed like you were making googly eyes at the panini shop earlier today."

She swatted his leg. "I was doing no such thing. At least, no more than you were," she said, lowering her voice to a tease. "Which means— I was absolutely, positively lusting over a sandwich."

A laugh shuddered through him. "That's what I thought, Happy Turtle."

"Let's do it, Tommy. Sounds like a perfect dinner spot."

While he'd happily take her to a fancier joint if she wanted, he was digging the fact that she was casual. She was easy. She didn't seem to require much when it came to creature comforts. He liked that in a woman. He wasn't a man who owned a tux. He didn't swirl wine or hit the links at a country club. He preferred beer, baseball, and boats, as well as sandwiches. After they arrived they ordered: Caribbean chicken for her and a spicy grouper sandwich for him, and beers for the both of them.

The faint tinkle of island music and the plink on the kettledrum wafted through the eatery, drifting onto the patio where they enjoyed a view of the inky black sea in the distance. She spread her napkin on her lap. "I've been thinking of something we talked about earlier on your deck. When you asked me earlier if I knew you," she began.

He nodded. "Go on."

"And I want to know more, Jake. Seems only fair. You've been to my happy place with me," she said, gesturing to the ocean that hugged the island. "Tell me more about your happy place."

He arched an eyebrow. "My happy place? You mean seats along the first baseline for the Marlins?"

She laughed, shaking her head. "Your family. They're your happy place, aren't they?"

He shot her a grin. "Yeah. They absolutely are."

She placed her hands on the table and leaned forward, listening. "Tell me about them."

This was easy. This was the easiest conversation in the world. Even though Kylie was a handful, and Brandt had been a wild child, they were *his*. He loved that she knew already that they were to him what the water was to her. His magic. He began with Kate, telling Steph about how it was his older sister's idea that he start the retrieval business when he returned from his stint in the army, then about how she liked to give him a hard time about anything and everything, including women. He liked to give her a hard time about her tabby cat, dubbed Inspector Cat, because he liked to knock mugs, flowers, pens, papers, earrings—anything he could get his paws on—off every surface in the house. "He's kind of an asshole, but then again, he *is* a cat."

"My mom has a cat like that. A tuxedo cat. She rips the toilet paper to shreds and eats the plants."

"Oh, she has an asshole cat, too?" he said drily.

"Is there any other kind?"

He shook his head. "Not that I can think of. But my nephew, Mason, loves that cat. Mason is pretty much the only person the cat is actually sweet to."

"What's Mason like?"

"He's a pistol. He's just like Brandt. The athlete of the bunch. Wild and playful. We used to say when Mason woke up, it was like a bomb going off. Kate's house went crazy with his energy. Brandt was like that, too, when he was younger, so it's kind of funny to see that in Mason now," he said.

She took a pull of her beer, then set it down on the red-checked tablecloth. "And what about Kylie? Why is she a handful, as you say?"

He scratched his jaw. "She's sweet but super scattered. She's always struggled a bit in school. She pulls through but needs extra help. Like in science and stuff. She's got a test coming up tomorrow and is a mess about it. She's got some anxiety issues, and it makes it harder for her to do well in school because of them."

Steph frowned. "That's too bad."

He nodded. "I wish it were easier for her, but honestly, I'm not sure it ever will be. She's had a rough time of school ever since our parents died, so my goal is just to get her through it."

"And it sounds like you're doing that," she said with a cheery note in her voice. "What about Brandt? Is he still the wild child?"

Jake smiled and shook his head, thinking of his kid brother and how much Brandt had changed over the years. "Nope. School settled him for some reason. He's intense and focused. He wants to be a lawyer and is applying to law school," he said, then winced briefly at the thought of the upcoming tuition bills that would start piling up. "That'll be a big chunk of change when he starts school."

"Law school isn't cheap."

"Don't I know it," he muttered.

She spread her fingers into a picture-frame shape. "The Jake picture is becoming clearer."

He cocked his head to the side. "How so?"

"That's the other reason why you're so driven, isn't it? Paying for their schools?"

Jake didn't delve into the details of his family with too many people. Family was private, and his job was the kind he preferred to keep on the down low. But he didn't seem to mind sharing the finer details of his life with Steph, for some reason. Perhaps because she was so different from Rosalinda. Steph's questions seemed to come from genuine interest, not from a need to know his weak spots. Rosalinda had had a hidden agenda. She'd peppered him with questions to unearth his vulnerabilities and learn when she could steal from him. Steph wasn't working for the enemy. Her motives were purely on the case and with him. She seemed to ask because she cared, and that made him open up.

"Yep. One hundred percent. They are all my reasons," he said, as a boisterous family entered the restaurant, waiting at the hostess stand. The noise pulled his attention briefly away from Steph, and for a second a flash of a sharp nose, the cut of a jawline, hanging by the edge of the waiting crowd, snapped into his memory. The profile felt familiar, but he wasn't sure why. Instinct told him to study the person, match the face to a name in his mental bank.

Then Steph spoke, softly and with a wide smile. "I love that you feel that way."

Like smoke wafting away, everything vanished but her, and he returned his attention to the woman across from him. She rested her chin in her hand, her gaze intently fixed on his. Her blue eyes were soft. "You really are like their father," she added.

When she said that, his damn heart beat harder and faster as it pounded against his chest. Like it was connecting to her because she not only *got* him, she was on the same wavelength.

The waitress arrived with their dinners, setting down the plates. After she left, Steph picked up her sandwich and returned to the conversation. "What kind of lawyer does Brandt want to be?"

"Prosecutor. He wants to save the world."

"Is that because of your parents and what happened to them?" she asked and took a bite of her panini.

"He doesn't want to see that happen again. He wants to do everything he can to fight back," he said, diving into his sandwich. Delicious.

"It's kind of amazing how you're both so driven by the same intense focus. But then it's not that surprising, either, I suppose. Is he like you in other ways?"

"Meaning is he charming, witty, and good-looking?"

She laughed. "Is he?"

"He is. I can say that about my little brother, right? He's a handsome bastard," he said, then grabbed his phone and scrolled to his photos. As they dined, he showed Steph several shots from his photo albums of the whole crew. His favorite people in the universe. As they finished, a note flashed on his screen from his little sister.

```
Almost ready for the test. I just have
one problem that's driving me crazy. It's
on frictional forces and I want to CRY.
```

Jake showed it to Steph. "See? This is what I mean about Kylie. Nervous wreck. Poor kid."

Steph furrowed her brow. "Is that for her physics test?"

He nodded.

She finished chewing, then set down the sandwich, took a drink, and said, "I won't pretend I'm a rocket scientist, but I know the answer to that. I could help her."

His eyes widened. "You could?"

She nodded enthusiastically. "I could and I would. Physics isn't the same as marine biology, but I was good in science so I can work my way through frictional forces. Want to call her and I can walk her through how to do that type of problem?"

"You're an angel," he said, and she beamed from the compliment.

His heart sped furiously with a giddy kind of excitement. With a surge of joy he hadn't felt in ages. He blinked, as if he could chase away this foreign feeling. But it was a good feeling, and it had no plans for departure. Happiness was lodging itself in that damn organ in his chest, which was terrifying and wonderful at the same damn time.

As she talked to Kylie, he tried to tell himself that he was simply relieved that his little sister was getting the help she badly needed. He made every effort to convince his brain that his heart wasn't hammering against his rib cage over the caring way Steph spoke to his sister, or how she'd talked about his siblings over dinner, or the genuine joy she'd shown from spending time in the ocean an hour ago.

Nope. His dumb heart couldn't possibly be fluttering for the woman. He was a smart man, and he knew better than to fall for a woman he worked with. Just to prove to himself that the bizarre sensations in his rib cage weren't anything more than admiration for his very temporary business partner, he thanked Steph in the way that mattered most to her—zeroing in on work. As she stepped away from the table for a quick ladies' room trip, he looked something up on his phone.

See? He did this because he cared about her as a one-time-only partner, not because he was feeling all sorts of crazy things for her.

Though as he wrote a few quick lines, he knew, he absolutely knew that he was lying to himself.

❦

As she stared in the mirror of the ladies' room, she willed her stomach to stop flipping. She tried to center herself with yoga mantras her mom espoused. To calm these escalating endorphins coursing through her veins that had her mind fast-forwarding to all sorts of dangerous possibilities with Jake.

Future possibilities.

Meeting his family. Getting to know the people he loved most. She shook her head. What on earth had gotten into her? Where had her reason and logic gone? Good Lord, how the heck could she be thinking of a down-the-road with the man who was after the only father she'd ever known?

She washed her hands, recalling how easy their conversation had been.

Somehow, the huge, massive misunderstanding that had nearly derailed them was now so far in the rearview mirror she couldn't even see it. She was cruising onward at a rapid pace, and they seemed to be growing closer.

How had *that* happened? This was supposed to be just business. They were supposed to be enjoying an island fling. She wasn't supposed to be *feeling*.

Maybe it was simply the time factor. The steady ticking of the clock as it marched toward the end of this trip surely was tricking her into believing something real was brewing between them. As she shut the faucet and grabbed a paper towel, she reminded herself that the ticking clock meant there was no time or space to become fond of the man.

Theirs was merely an arbitrary intimacy, borne of island breezes, too much sunshine, and being forced to share a room. None of the factors should lead to this rapidly beating heart; to the flushed cheeks; to the dopey, happy look in her eyes as she pictured more days and nights with him.

She shook a finger at her reflection.

Stay strong. Don't give in to all those butterflies.

She reminded herself Duke had promised to be good to her, and that had turned out to be a crock. Likewise, Jake had claimed he wouldn't turn in Eli, and she desperately longed to believe him, to blot out the memory of Duke's treachery and believe in a man's words. But really, how could she know for sure?

The only way to be certain was to keep her head on her shoulders and be guided by her brain.

She marched back to the table, a suit of metal donned, ready to protect herself. When she returned to his side, he shot her the sweetest smile. His soft lips curved up, his eyes crinkled at the corners, and they seemed to light up.

"What are you smiling about?" she asked, tilting her head to the side. A waitress walked around them, balancing a tray of sandwiches, beer, and iced tea. Jake held her gaze captive and gestured to the chair. "Sit down. I have something to show you."

She parked herself in the chair as he showed her the screen on his phone.

It was open to a TripAdvisor page about Ariel's Island Eco-Adventure Tours. A new review had landed on her listing. As she started reading, a smile spread across her face. So wide she was unsure she could contain it—not as she read words like *great customer service, incredible dive leader, brilliant knowledge of marine life, super nice woman running the business.*

They were simple words, but thrilling ones.

They meant the world to her. Not because she was jonesing for one more review. But because he'd done it, knowing it mattered to her, it reversed the hurt. So much for her suit of armor. He couldn't be more different than her ex. She set down the phone, leaned across the table, cupped his cheeks in her hands, and kissed him. Soft at first, but in seconds it climbed the ladder and turned feverish. Her skin sizzled, and she murmured as the kiss consumed her. He groaned as their tongues tangled in the kind of heated kiss that could turn into a furious duet of longing. She was vaguely aware of the diners and her own sense of propriety, so she sealed her lips tightly to his, kissed him hard one final time, then let go.

"Thank you," she said as she sat back down. "Even though you've never done one of my tours, that was very sweet."

"I beg to differ. I have done one of your tours," he said with a playful rise in his eyebrow. "Tonight."

"Was that an official or unofficial tour?"

"Unofficial, unpaid, who cares? I had the time of my life and I want everyone to know Ariel's Island Eco-Adventure Tours is the best in the business."

"You know what you deserve for that amazing review?"

"An epic blowjob? A chance to put you on all fours and sink into you?" he asked.

OK fine. Ripping off clothes was quite fun, and she didn't want that factor to disappear. She laughed. "You are such a dirty bastard."

"I am, and you love it."

"I do, and you'll get all of that, but I was thinking ice cream right now."

"That works, too."

He tossed the napkin on the table in a rush, held out his hand, and eagerly walked with her to the nearest ice-cream stand.

Holding hands. The entire way. Squeezing her fingers. Running the pad of his thumb absently over the top of her hand.

Kissing was good, sex was fantastic, but holding hands?

That was magical. And it brought a return of those damn butterflies, and all the future possibilities.

Dangerous things, butterflies. Scarier than jewel thieves.

CHAPTER ELEVEN

The mint chip was delicious. The company was even better. The taste of sweetness on her lips as he kissed her one more time, as they walked along the street, music playing from bars, the island breeze floating by, was the best.

As the sign for the Pink Pelican flickered neon in the night, Jake tipped his forehead to the bar where they'd first met several nights ago. "Quick game of darts before we call it a night?"

"You're a glutton for punishment," she said, then fixed on her best game face. "Get ready to be destroyed, Harlowe."

"You're on."

But this time he won. He raised his arms in victory as he defeated her.

She frowned as Marie scurried from one end of the bar to another, tending to customers. "No fair. Another round?"

"Not 'til you admit I beat the dart master fair and square," he said.

She scowled. "Never. I will never admit defeat."

He grabbed her waist and slammed her close. Her breath caught. He nipped her earlobe. "Admit it," he growled. "Admit I am masterful at darts. Then, and only then, will I accept your rematch offer."

She shook her head and made a move to reach for the dart in his hand. Like she was trying to subtly snatch it away. He clamped his palm around it and raised an eyebrow. "You trying to pickpocket me?"

"If pickpocketing from your hand counts, then yes. I was."

"You need a lesson in proper pickpocketing then, woman. You're too obvious. Like you were in the alley earlier today."

"You're telling me you know how to pick pockets, too?" She narrowed her eyes, skepticism in her tone as she grabbed her iced tea from the nearby counter and took a drink.

He laughed. "I do. I don't do it often, but it's a useful skill."

She put down the glass, then parked her hands on her hips, hiking up her purse on her shoulder. "Teach me."

"Can't really teach you everything in one night, but it's all about the art of deception," he said as he led her back to the dartboard. Grabbing a dart from the green felt, he raised it and took aim at the bull's-eye. Her gaze followed the dart. "That means you need to get the person to look elsewhere, like at the dartboard."

She nodded and stared at the dartboard. For one second. Two seconds. Three.

Then it dawned on her. When she snapped her focus back to him, he brandished her wallet. "You got that from my purse," she said, stomping a foot.

"I sure did. But that was the point. To show you how it's done."

"OK," she said, wiggling her fingers. "Let me try."

He taught her a few basic distraction tricks, and she practiced on him, dipping her hands in his pockets and trying to pilfer his watch. She was no pro, and he was aware of her moves every time. But her technique improved with the brief lesson. However, the constant gliding of her hands into his pockets zapped his focus away from teaching and onto the next phase of tonight.

"That's all for today's lesson," he said, since he had no more interest in being out with her. "Need to get you alone now."

Her eyes told him she wanted that, too.

"Let's say good night to Marie." She'd been busy all evening pulling the tap and pouring drinks, so he drummed his fingertips against the bar, tipped an imaginary hat to her, and waved good-bye.

But she beckoned them over.

"Hey. You found your sexy fisherman," Marie said to Steph, flicking her long braid off her shoulder so it hung down her back. She turned to Jake. "And you found my favorite mermaid."

"We did find each other," Steph said in a sweet voice that nailed him right in the heart.

We found each other.

Those words. They pulsed with double meaning.

But before he could linger any more on the way his heart freaking skipped from hearing them, an awareness dawned on him. Like a light-bulb of obviousness turning on. Marie might know something about the burglary. She might have seen something. Her bar was located a few shops away from the gallery. He seized the moment and gestured for her to come closer. "Did you hear about the robbery down the street last night?" he asked, whispering so the other patrons wouldn't hear. "Heard a diamond walked off."

"I did," she said. "They had a big old party at the gallery. But by the end of the party, Isla's diamond had disappeared. They're trying to keep it quiet, but it's obvious she's wearing a fake now."

"You think someone at the party stole Isla's diamond?"

Marie shrugged. "Who knows? Has to be, right?"

"Who was there?"

"Everyone. The assistant manager. The manager. The realtor. The guy with the snake tattoo," she said, then a new customer sidled up to the bar and raised a few fingers, eager to order.

"Need to run," Marie said and blew them a kiss. "Come back soon." Then she stopped in her tracks and leaned across the counter. "You two make an adorable couple. You know that, right?"

Steph blushed, and Jake stammered a thanks.

As they left, Steph squeezed his arm. "Snake tattoo," she whispered when they reached the sidewalk. "The assistant manager at the nightclub."

Jake's memory was jogged. He'd seen the guy in Eli's office at the nightclub the other night. Had he been in the office legitimately? Or was he poking around? "Think he's our Mr. Smith?"

"He knows Eli. He'd probably know Eli had some diamonds. He certainly knew Isla had one. What if he took it last night at the party? Maybe he has a bone to pick with Eli." Her eyes widened, and she grabbed his arm, clutching him tightly. "I saw him at Happy Turtle a few days ago. He was sunbathing and looked like he was asleep. But what if he was . . ."

"Following you?"

She nodded, her face whiter than it had been a moment before.

"We'll keep our eyes peeled for him. And you're seeing Eli tomorrow, right?"

She nodded as a night breeze drifted by, swirling the hem of her skirt. "I am. I'll see what I can find out. I have an idea for how to pull off the next phase."

On the walk back to the hotel, they plotted the next day. As they headed through the front doors of the hotel, he dropped a kiss to her cheek. "So much better to work with you than against you," he whispered.

"I can think of other things you can do against me, too," she said, wiggling her eyebrows.

He groaned, low and husky, his arm tightening around her shoulders as they moved through the crowds in the lobby. His hotel was bigger than hers and nicer, too, with a wide-open lobby, bar, and sleek floors. Music from a live band drifted from the busy bar and Steph glanced briefly at the throngs of people drinking, laughing, singing along.

As they reached the elevator, she spotted a woman with jet-black hair, twisted in a bun, perched on a barstool. Familiarity tugged at her as Steph pushed the button, but focusing was hard when Jake's hands were on her waist, his lips brushing soft kisses on her neck.

"That woman . . . I think she's . . ."

Oh. His lips were right there on the shell of her ear. Her eyes floated closed.

"What were you saying?" he whispered.

"Looks familiar," she said, her voice hazy from his touch. "I saw her at Isla's house."

He cast a disinterested gaze in the direction of the bar, just as the elevator doors whisked open. She wasn't the guy with the snake tattoo. He wasn't worried.

He held up his hands like a seesaw, moving each palm up and down. "Bar. Room. Bar. Room."

He tugged her into the elevator before the doors closed.

The choice was made.

CHAPTER TWELVE

Sharing a hotel room could be awkward. Would your habits align? Would he be messy and you neat? Would he leave smelly socks on the air conditioner or play the TV too loud?

None of those things had happened so far.

But staying in the same space with a new lover was already fraught with peril during daylight. At night? Even odder. Darkness and a bed spelled surefire romance, but would the forced intimacy be too much to bear? Would they brush their teeth, wash their faces, and turn off the lights? Peck on the cheek, roll over, and go to sleep?

Ah, who was she kidding?

She'd be shocked if they went to bed for bed. The two of them had never been terribly good at keeping hands to themselves. In the past, though, they'd had excuses to erect stop signs.

Tonight, in the same room, there were no more roadblocks.

But rather than guess when the moment would begin or who would initiate, she took the bull by the horns once the door clicked shut behind them. Because she wanted him. She wanted to make the most of these three nights with him. She wanted to wring every last drop of passion from this fling.

"I'm glad to be staying with you tonight," she said as she wrapped her arms around his neck, brushing her fingertips along his skin.

He pretended to yawn, big and loud. "What did you say? I'm tired. I think I'm going to fall asleep."

"Oh no you're not." She reached for his shirt collar and gripped it, holding him close.

"Why not?"

"You were all frisky in the elevator, and I have plans for you."

"The last time you had plans for me, I wound up blindfolded. That your MO again?"

"No, but you're close," she said, then turned around, walked to her suitcase, and rummaged through it to locate the wrap she'd used that afternoon. He'd wandered to the middle of the room, and she folded it over and placed it in his hands.

He raised an eyebrow in question.

"Do what you want to me with it," she said softly. Nerves thrummed through her. She'd never had kinky sex, and while blindfolding wasn't the height of wildness, she was eager to explore new terrain with Jake. She sensed he had a sexually adventurous side, that he'd try nearly anything.

"You want me to blindfold you? So you can't see what I'm doing to you?"

"If you want," she said, offering herself to him. "I trust you."

"You do?"

He stepped closer and ran his finger along her cheek. It was his gesture. His signature touch. He always seemed to do that to connect with her. As if it signaled when moments shifted from mere carnality to something deeper.

"I do."

He tossed the wrap behind him on the bed. In a flash, he tugged her dress over her head, then dropped it in a navy-and-white puddle on the floor.

"You're fast," she said. "You must really want payback."

"I'm not going to blindfold you," he said, then bent his head to her neck and pressed a hot kiss to her collarbone. She trembled, loving his kisses, seeking more of them. He blazed a path up the column of her throat, making her squirm in his arms. He ran his hands along the bare flesh of her arms, from her shoulders to her wrists to her waist. Traveling up her back, he unhooked her bra, letting the white silk fall to the ground.

"You're not?"

He shook his head as he cupped her breasts in his big hands. She moaned. Goose bumps rose on her flesh as he kneaded them, running the pads of his thumbs over her hard nipples. She melted from his touch. Her whole body turned white-hot, and the craving intensified. Multiplied. "Nope. Not gonna use it to cover your eyes."

Other possibilities danced before her, and the prospects turned her on more. So did the anticipation. He dropped his mouth to one breast, drew in her nipple, and sucked gently.

She murmured and sighed, her hands seeking the back of his head, her fingers finding his hair as she held him close and he kissed and licked her breast, sending her into a frenzy. She was ready for him to take her, to toss her on the bed and do anything.

But he let go of her breast and raised an eyebrow, his eyes shining with mischief.

She looked at him expectantly, but he said nothing. Instead, he wasted no time moving on to his own clothes. After stripping off his shirt, he backed up, his knees hitting the mattress. He flopped down on it, then scooted up to a pillow, propping himself on it. He tucked another pillow under his head, giving himself a view.

Of her.

Excitement rippled through her as he raked his gaze over her from head to toe. She was nearly naked, and on display for him. The bulge in his shorts grew bigger as he roamed his eyes along her frame from his spot on the bed.

She ran her hand from her breasts down to her belly. "Like what you see?"

"Very much," he said roughly. "I'd like it more if you'd take off that last little item that's in the way of my unobstructed view."

She dipped a thumb into the waistband of her panties, teasing, taking it slow. Lowering one side an inch. Then the other. Just a little farther now. Enough for a peekaboo of what he wanted. He sighed deeply in appreciation, then stroked his hard-on through his shorts. "Love what I see. Fucking love it. Look what you're doing to me," he said, his voice husky as he touched himself.

She bit her lip as heat raced through her. She was burning up just from looking at him on his bed like that. Aroused. He was so sexy all the time, but especially now, when he was nothing but lust and desire.

The lights were dim, the sliding glass door was open, and the curtains blew gently in the breeze. The sound of waves lapping the shore was the sound track to this moment as she toyed with her underwear. His eyes blazed darkly, narrowing as he stared heavy-lidded at her impromptu strip show.

"Take them off. All the way off," he growled.

She sashayed her hips back and forth once more, a final tease. Then, since he was running the show, she pushed her panties to her ankles and stepped out of them. "Fuck," he rasped out as he blinked and stared. Just fucking stared. Practically eating her up with his hungry gaze. "Get over here."

She walked to the bed and crawled across the mattress to him on her hands and knees. He patted his chest. "Come closer. Climb on me. Sit on my face," he said, his voice low and dirty, and her skin sizzled. Everywhere. She was flush with desire, thrilling at his commands. Something about this man hooked into her—it was physical but rapidly barreling down a path toward more. He made her laugh, he made her think, he challenged her, and he accepted no bullshit. He required only honesty in everything, and it was such a wondrous thing after the time she'd given to her ex to be with someone who craved truth. After Duke and Eli, she'd learned not to trust easily. But Jake was showing her new ways to trust.

Including this kind of trust in bed. Shooting out an arm, he grabbed the wrap from the bed, then dangled it as she inched over him. He patted his shoulder with his other hand. "Higher now," he said in a naughty tone. "I need you straddling me."

Her breath came hard and fast before she even reached his shoulders. He grabbed her hips and held her in place, kneeling her over his face.

"Steph," he said in the softest voice, but one that brooked no argument.

"Yes?" she asked, swallowing thickly.

He gripped her wrists in one hand and tugged them behind her back. "I don't want to blindfold you. Know why?"

"Why?" she asked, a pulse beating insistently between her legs. She needed his touch. Needed his tongue. Needed some kind of wild contact to quench her desire.

"Because of your eyes," he said as he gripped her wrists and wrapped the fabric around them.

"What about them?"

"I love looking at you when you come. When you're close. When you're getting there," he said, and she gasped as a fresh wave of desire crashed into her. Like a wave slamming the shore. He wasn't even touching her, and she ached with longing. An exquisite, insistent ache between her legs. She was going to go off like a rocket tonight, she was sure. As she straddled his face, she took the power position, yet he had all the control as he tightened the knot around her bound wrists, securing her hands behind her back.

"I like it when you look at me, Jake," she said in a feathery whisper.

"That's why blindfolding you would be a crime," he said, then lowered her wetness to his mouth, and she moaned a staccato sound of pleasure. Because . . . holy fuck.

His tongue felt so good.

His talented tongue stroked a sizzling line across her sex. Then, he flicked her with the tip, and her quick breaths turned into pants. "Soooo good, so good." She moaned, her eyes floating closed.

As the world behind her lids turned dark, she wobbled for the briefest moment. Not much, maybe an inch. But the precariousness of the position hit her. She had nothing to hold on to. She was going to ride his face without reins. She couldn't use her hands to brace against the wall. She opened her eyes. He was looking right at her.

"I've got you," he whispered, holding her hips tight.

She nodded, letting go, giving in.

Another cry fell from her lips as he worked his tongue in a frenzied circle across her. Pleasure forked in her, blasting through every cell. Her belly tingled. Her skin burned. Her cheeks reddened from all this incomparable heat. Every inch of her was aflame. Even her toes were turned on. She went wild and crazy on his wicked tongue, his magic mouth, his stubbled chin. He was her launching pad to pleasure, and she was taking off.

She could barely focus on one thing, but she was keenly aware that he never looked away. He kept his gaze on her face, her parted lips, her eyes.

It no longer mattered that her hands were bound. Even as some primal instinct told her to slam her palms against the wall to hold on, she didn't need to. Because he had her. He had her pleasure thoroughly mastered with his mouth, and that was all she needed to fly over the cliff. Her orgasm flooded his lips as she came hard on his face.

"Oh God, oh God, oh God," she shouted, then chased it with a chorus of moans and groans. She couldn't stop trembling. Couldn't stop coming. She squeezed her eyes shut. Keeping them open was too hard, too intense. She rode out the waves as the aftershocks of a mind-blowing climax vibrated in her bones.

Soon, he lifted her off him, untied her wrists, placed her on her back, and raised her arms over her head. Then retied them. "Stay like that," he told her.

Like she was going anywhere else.

∽

He shucked off his shorts and briefs, his erection slapping his belly. He rolled on a condom, his shaft aching to be inside her. She was so beautiful, her hair fanning out on the bed, her skin flushed, her eyes glossy with pleasure.

She radiated sexiness.

"Spread your legs for me," he said.

As she parted her legs, he nearly came right there. The sight of her aroused like this stoked the flames inside him. He wanted more of her pleasure. He loved driving her wild. He savored hearing her noises. She was so free in bed, and that was what he wanted. A lover who had no inhibitions, who trusted, who took and who gave, and who opened herself up.

Her.

He wanted her.

He positioned himself at her entrance, rubbed the head against her, and eased inside.

"Jesus," he said as he sank into her.

She clenched around him, arching her back.

Sparks tore through him from the hot feel of her. His blood was on fire. His lust was a force of nature and it overwhelmed him with its intensity, rippling through his blood and bones. She felt amazing, and she looked stunning with her arms bound above her head, her back bowed, her red lips falling open in an *O*. He lowered himself to his elbows, bringing his chest to hers. Then he moved inside her, building a slow, steady rhythm. He could come in seconds if he went hard and fast, but he wanted this time to last. Wanted to experience every single rapturous moment of being inside her. Especially when she was already blissed out. Warm and pliant, she had that buzzed, sex-drunk look in her blue eyes.

"You look so beautiful," he rasped out.

"So do you."

He swiveled his hips and pushed into her. She answered him by wrapping her legs tightly around his ass, her heels digging in to pull him deeper.

Yeah, that's what he wanted. To bury himself inside her. To reach the magic spot in her. She rocked with him, circling her hips, her lips falling open and her breath erratic. Her wild sounds and her sexy cries that rose higher and higher told him he could do it again. He could take her to the edge one more time. They had that kind of chemistry, that kind of heat. He rose up on his knees, grasped her rear, and pulled her closer, finding a deeper angle.

One that sent pleasure crackling down his spine. Like he'd been ignited.

She writhed.

"Oh God," she cried, and that was enough for him to know she was on her way. But he wanted to be closer. He wanted her arms around him as he came. Her nails digging into him. Her sweet, lush body as close as she could be. In a blur, he quickly unknotted her wrists as he fucked her. "Need your arms around me," he muttered, pressing his chest to hers.

In seconds, she was free, and she flung her arms around his back. "Yeah, like that," he said, and his throat was dry, and his climax was looming around the corner. Ready to work its way through his body. To tear through him in a storm of lust.

She curled her fingers into his shoulders and gripped her thighs tight to his ass.

He drove into her and he was there, and she was there, moaning and writhing and finding another release beneath him as he came inside the woman he was crazy for.

∽

He held her in his arms, planting kisses on her neck, her hair, her shoulders. He was sure now. He was certain. He didn't want this affair with her to end. He wanted it to go on and on. Like they were a couple. Like Marie had said. Because they were so damn good together.

As she fell asleep in his arms, the stars winking through the windows, this moment felt like it had the potential to be endless. Like it could stretch on and on into this pure connection with another person.

The trouble was, he couldn't sleep. Something nagged at him. Or really, two things. Two moments from tonight. Once, at the restaurant when he should have focused harder on the sharp profile at the edge of the crowd. Then, here at the hotel, when he should have checked out the woman in the lobby. He hadn't even bothered to address Steph's concern.

He'd been solely interested in getting her in bed.

He stroked his hand along her hair, wishing, hoping that these feelings for her weren't threatening his focus on work.

He'd once thought getting involved with a woman on a job meant he'd be crossed. But what if it meant he'd lose his edge?

As he dragged his fingers through her soft strands, he promised himself that he'd do better tomorrow.

CHAPTER THIRTEEN

Showtime.

She walked along the block to Eli's club at eleven fifteen the next morning. Today, she was the gun and she was the sniper.

Though truth be told, there was no need for a weapon, except the tool she had in her purse, slung on her shoulder. No watchman required, either.

That was one of the benefits of being the inside woman on a job. She didn't need someone to stand guard for her. She could stand as her own lookout. Her position as the stepdaughter was all she required to surprise Eli. Their scheduled lunch wasn't for another forty-five minutes, which meant she'd likely be able to find him now at one of his favorite spots. He'd told her at their first brunch that he was at Sapphire most days.

Her green shades covered her eyes, blocking out the bright sun. Not a cloud dared appear in the perfect crystal-blue sky. No wonder Eli had chosen the Cayman Islands for his new life. This land was the definition of paradise, and the balmy air caressed her bare skin as the island breezes drifted by. Funny how the weather forecast on her app had predicted today would be a scorcher, but it was wrong—today was another day in paradise. She wore a pink sundress, flip-flop sandals with a shell design on the straps, and a pair of delicate mermaid earrings—quirky but pretty. Jake's hotel wasn't far away, so she'd chosen to walk, rather than drive, to the club.

Sapphire loomed closer, its appearance different during the day. No flashing lights beckoning to tourists, no cool blue neon sign luring those out for the evening, no velvet rope holding back teeming throngs of island partiers. Just a gray front door and one security guard manning it. The guy wore aviator shades and had his arms crossed. He stood stock-still as he surveyed the block.

Steph headed up the steps and greeted the guard. "Hi. I'm Steph Anderson. I'm here to see Eli."

His blank expression disappeared and a smile spread. "Good to see you again. Welcome back. Mr. Thompson is in his office," the man said, pushing a beefy palm against the heavy steel door. He gestured for her to go inside.

As she entered the quiet Sapphire, it was as if she'd wandered into a Halloween haunted house with all the lights flicked on, its secrets revealed. Regular fluorescent lights glowed overhead, illuminating the bar, the floor, the stage, the balcony. The flashing colors and techno-heavy music were absent. No hum of crowds, no clink of glasses. The slinky, sexy, sultry mood of after hours was gone. The club did its best impression of a warehouse, big and echoey, as Steph's sandals slapped across the tiles. As she neared the winding staircase at the edge of the dance floor, a flash of bright yellow appeared at the top of the steps.

"Steph!"

She craned her neck upward to find Clarissa waving to her. Her father's assistant manager flew down the steps in a banana-yellow dress, her dark hair like a sheet, her high heels clacking.

"Cal told me you were here," Clarissa said as she neared the bottom step.

Steph furrowed her brow.

"At the front door. He's our security guard," she explained. "He buzzed me that you were here. Eli's in his office working, but he's been practically bouncing off the walls with excitement to see you again."

That piqued Steph's curiosity. Did Eli talk about her that much? "He mentioned we were having lunch?" she asked as Clarissa swiveled around and headed toward the stairs.

The assistant manager nodded. "He's been in the most joyous mood all week since you arrived. This very morning he told me he was counting down the minutes 'til he saw you."

"I'm excited to see him, too."

And his artwork. I'm incredibly excited to see that.

"He's so proud of you, and all that you've accomplished. He told me you had a scuba tour later this week. How exciting. Where will you take them?"

Steph rattled off the itinerary for her upcoming tour—the visit to the Bloody Bay site, then to Little Cayman.

"I love all those places. I'd love to join the tour and do a little diving."

"Oh, you should. I've got room if you want to," Steph said.

"I'll do that. I have the day off so I should be able to come along. And are you otherwise enjoying your time in our island paradise?" Clarissa asked as they neared the top of the steps.

Enjoying was one way to put it. *Savoring* worked, too. *Coming every night* was another phrase. A flicker of desire stirred in her belly as Steph rewound to twelve hours ago in Jake's bed. "I'm having the time of my life," Steph said, a private little grin curving her lips as she thought of her roomie, her partner, her temporary lover.

A parade of images flashed before her eyes—bending over the railing on the balcony, kissing Jake at the panini shop, reading his review, diving under the ocean with him. From the dirty to the sweet, everything with the sexy, funny, witty, caring Jake Harlowe was so damn good.

Her foot landed awkwardly on the next step. Grabbing the railing, she caught herself before she toppled down the stairs.

Thinking about the man she liked was damn distracting.

Liked.

Well, duh. She knew she liked him, but *liked* seemed far too tame for that swirl of emotions that had nearly knocked her over. *Was it more than like?*

"Are you OK?" Clarissa asked, eyes wide.

Steph bent to adjust her flip-flop, trying to make light of her near face-plant. "I knew I shouldn't have put sunscreen on the soles of my feet, too," she said as she rose.

Clarissa laughed. "I'm glad you're OK. And I'm equally glad you're having a lovely stay." She lowered her voice and wagged her finger playfully. "But don't let on to Eli how much fun you're having, or he'll try to convince you to live here. He'd be beside himself with glee if you moved to the Islands."

Steph flashed a brief smile, resuming her pace up the steps. "The Caymans is a great place to live, but Miami is pretty awesome, too. Where are you from?"

"Here. But I went to college in North Carolina and had hoped to stay after graduation. Had some trouble finding work like everyone else finishing college these days, so I decided to come back to the Caymans and try my luck here at home."

"And it sounds like luck has been on your side?"

She knocked on the railing. "Knock on wood. Yes, it has. I love my job here, and Eli is good to me. If you ever change your mind and move here, you'd make Mr. Thompson the happiest person on earth." Clarissa resumed her pace up the steps. "Then again, the man is already pretty much the happiest guy I know," she added with a cheery shrug.

This was the Eli she knew and loved. This was who she wanted him to be. The good guy, the generous guy, the guy who brought jobs to locals, who gave to charity, who loved her.

How could he possibly be the man who had stolen so much from so many? There had to be another explanation. Someone else must be behind the missing money. Hell, maybe that luxury goods merchant was the mastermind and was simply trying to pin it on Eli. Maybe Eli's diamonds were legitimately earned, and the merchant had simply made it look like Eli procured them from ill-gotten gains. If she could find the diamonds, she could help solve the crime.

"Happiest guy on earth. That describes Eli Thompson to a *T*," Steph said as they reached the balcony that wrapped around the dance floor. As she turned the corner down the hallway, she heard his voice on the phone, carrying through the open door. "Perfect. So glad the deal is working out. She'll simply be thrilled," he said, and Steph wondered briefly who he was talking about, and which deal was coming together.

When they reached his office, Clarissa pressed the door open all the way. Eli's back was to them. Immediately, Steph snapped her attention to the art on the walls. She sighed quietly in relief. Only one frame hung, and it didn't look too heavy. She could do this—aim and shoot.

She patted her purse absently as Eli turned around in his chair.

When his blue eyes landed on her, they twinkled. He waved broadly. His lips curved in a huge grin.

Steph's gut twisted. This was going to be easy. For all the wrong reasons. She was about to use his emotions to hoodwink him. Just as he'd done to her mother for all those years. Telling her he loved her, then lying behind her back.

But it was for the best, she reminded herself. She was going to find the diamonds for the greater good. For everyone.

She lifted her chin and walked inside, head up high.

❦

All business. Jake was like a laser the next morning. His focus on the case was razor sharp. He had his mission, and he was sticking to it. No distractions allowed.

The bell above the door jingled as Jake entered Uncut. He scanned quickly for Wilder, the gentleman who'd helped him a few days ago. From his post behind the glass display counter, the man presented a diamond necklace to a woman wearing a white tennis skirt and a visor.

"Beautiful, isn't it? And it goes with everything," he said.

The woman shook her head, mouthed a thanks, and turned on her heels to go. Wilder returned the necklace to the case. Jake ambled over to the dark-haired man, who beamed as he looked up. He shook his index finger at Jake several times. "Who's the man?"

Jake pointed two thumbs at himself. "Am I the man?"

"You are the man indeed. At last, I beat my brother in darts." Wilder raised his arms in victory. "Thanks to your angle trick. I am so grateful."

"Excellent. Does that mean I get a free diamond now for my sister?" he asked with a wink.

The man laughed loudly and clasped his hand on his belly. "Oh, that's rich. You are a funny man."

"So that's a no?" he said drily.

"That would be a big, fat no," Wilder said, but his tone was playful. "Are you ready to buy for her? For her new job? A diamond would be lovely."

Jake heaved a sigh. "I might be. Someday. But listen, man. I gotta come clean to you." He was going out on a limb here, but Wilder had been a decent guy when Jake first talked to him. If he was going to pump him for information, the least he could do was offer up some truth.

Wilder's expression shifted to one of concern and curiosity. "What is it?"

Jake took off his sunglasses and met his eyes. "A woman I know—a woman I'm close with," he added, because it was true, "had her diamond stolen from her hotel room here on the island. Those blue-tinted ones we talked about."

Wilder's eyes widened. "Oh dear. I don't like to hear about diamond thefts. It makes me sad when diamonds are not with their rightful owners."

"Yeah, me, too. So I'm just wondering," he said, reaching into his pocket and taking out his phone. "If you've seen this guy around at all." Jake opened to a saved photo of Ferdinand, the guy with the snake tattoo. He'd snagged it from the Sapphire website that morning. Jake wasn't sure if Ferdinand was the thief, but given Marie's tip last night, coupled with Steph spotting him earlier on the trip and Jake's run-in at the club office, he might as well start with Eli's manager. "Trying to figure out if this guy's been trying to turn that blue diamond back into money."

Wilder tensed and pointed to the screen. "I've seen him around," he said in a nervous whisper.

"You have?" Excitement zipped through Jake. "Where? When?"

Wilder waved frantically toward the door. "Yesterday. He was at a café nearby with the man who runs International Diamonds."

Jake nearly pumped his fist. "Really?"

"And everyone here knows International Diamonds turns the blue diamonds. He probably went straight there with the gem."

"Yeah, he probably did," Jake said, and this new intel placed the man with the snake tattoo at the head of the line as Suspect Number One. "Anything else you saw at the café? Did you hear anything?"

Wilder shook his head, his eyes etched with worry. "No. I was just walking by on my way back from lunch." Wilder paused, tilted his head.

"But I thought perhaps he was working for Mr. Thompson. Since he works for him at Sapphire."

Shit.

Jake's hopes plummeted as it hit him—the man might be totally legit. He could be working the diamond trade on behalf of Eli. Ferdinand might have been meeting with International Diamonds as Eli's middleman, rather than to peddle his own stolen gem. It was entirely possible that Ferdinand was helping Eli turn his diamonds into cash and vice versa, rather than pilfering diamonds from the women Eli cared about—Steph and Isla.

Jake's shoulders sagged. He was right where he started a few minutes ago. Circling suspects. Trying to figure out who had stolen Steph's diamond, and therefore, who was after the other hundreds of sparkly gems.

"Thanks, man," he said, and held out a hand to shake.

When Jake left the shop, he took a minute to recalibrate, weighing next steps. He needed more information, so he called Kate and gave her three names.

"I'll have intel for you in an hour," she said in her crisp, business tone.

"Excellent," he said. "Tell Mason I'm bringing him back a new snorkel mask and we're going to dive for buried treasure off the coast of Key Largo."

Kate laughed. "He'll be excited. He misses you," she said, down-shifting to a softer voice now.

"I miss the little guy, too."

A few minutes later, he wandered along Wayboard Street, passing International Diamonds. He peered inside, scanning for the woman who'd helped him last week. Monica was her name. Maybe he could poke around somehow, see what she knew. She'd given him useful information on the value of the diamonds and where they came from in Canada. She could be a valuable resource about the two new missing gems and who was trying to sell them. But, as he started to formulate a game plan, he recalled how she'd seemed a touch suspicious of him.

He didn't see her inside the shop.

Perhaps that was for the best. No need to stir up the hornet's nest with her. He left the diamond district and headed toward Tristan's. He needed a quiet spot to dial Steph at the appointed time. He'd pay a visit to the restaurant, poke around and see what he could learn about the proprietor, then slip into the restroom to call Steph at eleven thirty.

Yep, he had his edge back. He was firing on all cylinders today.

As he bounded up the steps, the hair on the back of his neck tingled. He had the distinct sensation of being followed. Whipping his head around, he spotted a flash of dark hair in a tight bun. He rushed back down the steps. The woman had whisked into a dress store.

A woman who looked a lot like Monica.

A recent memory slammed to the front of his brain. Holy shit. He'd spotted her the other night at the bar on the beach, where Steph had enjoyed the Cherry Popsicle. He'd gone there with her after the party at Isla and Eli's house.

Was the diamond saleswoman following him?

CHAPTER FOURTEEN

Eli plunked down the receiver with a flourish.

He opened his arms for a hug, but then furrowed his brow. He raised his wrist to look at the face of his Rolex. "Wait. Am I late for lunch? Did I get the time wrong?"

Steph waved off his concern and flashed a big, bright smile. "Nope. I'm just early. I was doing some shopping in the neighborhood and thought I would pop in to see you in your element."

Her stomach churned as she lied about the reason for her early arrival.

Eli strode across the plum-colored carpet of his office and wrapped her in a big embrace. "You should stay in the Caymans," he declared with a happy sigh, then broke the hug. "Sit," he said, patting a plush black leather couch.

"Is there a conspiracy going on to get me to relocate here?" she teased. "Clarissa said the same thing."

"Smart woman. That's why I keep her around. I told her to convince you."

She laughed, but the chuckle didn't sound as if it came from her. It seemed to originate from another Steph—one who was playing pretend, who was imitating a woman who felt no guilt. Steph wasn't terribly acquainted with that version of herself. She hadn't played her before. "Clarissa was definitely convincing, but I don't think a move is in the cards. I like Miami—and Mom—too much," she said, because at least that was wholly true. "I hope I'll be here more often, though. I had some inquiries about snorkel tours and a visit to Happy Turtle, so fingers crossed."

He raised his index and middle finger, twisting them together. "Good. Nothing could make me happier than seeing you around more often. Now tell me about your shopping trip. What did you see? What did you buy?" he asked, peering around as if hunting for bags.

Shoot. Why hadn't she brought props for every wrinkle in her lie? Lying was hard. It required too much advance prep.

Think, think.

Her right thumb and index finger darted to her ear. "These earrings," she said, fastening on a bright smile as she leaned forward to show him her mermaid earrings. "Aren't they cute?"

"*Cute* is the wrong word," he said, his expression serious. "They are beautiful. Isla would love them. She loves pretty little earrings."

Of course she does. She loves shiny objects. She's probably the mastermind.

"Where did you get them?"

A make-believe store I just invented from thin air.

"Oh, just a tiny boutique in Georgetown," she said breezily, naming a popular shopping area.

"Which one? I want to get her a pair."

She stared at the ceiling. Scrunched up her brow. Scratched her chin. "Darn. I can't seem to remember the name. We were only there for a little while before we came over here to do some window shopping," she said, feeling a bit like she was on the hot seat, so she quickly shifted gears. "You know, save money and all. I went with my friend Tommy. He's helping me on my tour in a few days."

"Ah, how lovely," Eli said casually. But Steph was comprised of tense muscles and tight skin as she waited for a phone call from "Tommy." "Is this Tommy fellow a nice guy?"

She nodded. "Very nice. He's checking on some of the equipment we need for the tour. That should keep him occupied for a few hours this afternoon. He needs to stay busy, since his girlfriend just broke up with him, and he's still heartbroken. So he likes the extra work to keep his mind off her."

Eli nodded, an intensely serious look on his face. "Of course. There's nothing like hard work to distract a man from heartache."

"But that gives me plenty of time with you," she said, clasping his hand and squeezing it, laying the foundation for her own smoke and mirrors that would come any minute. Eleven thirty ticked closer.

"Why don't we leave early and pop into Isla's gallery? Then I'll drive us over to the restaurant," he suggested, and her heart skittered with worry. Driving with him was fine, but she couldn't leave early. She needed to wait for that call. Her ears perked, longing to hear the phone trill any second.

She just had to keep him occupied until it rang.

"I keep meaning to check out the Lynx paintings. And oh," she said, pointing to the square design on the wall. "You have one, too." She feigned excitement as she focused on staying put in his office, rather than leaving for Isla's gallery. "Isla said you're both huge fans of his work."

"Isn't it gorgeous? We love his concept of the world. Oh, and he sent lunch to Isla yesterday. What a treat! When she called his office to leave a message to thank him, his assistant sounded a little surprised at first, as if she hadn't known he sent it. But he's on a meditation retreat, so she probably assumed he would be too busy focusing on the sound of waves or the falling of rain or some such to be thinking about others. But that's just the type of kind man he is!"

Steph fought back a smirk. "How thoughtful."

"Too bad you weren't able to join Isla and her staff to enjoy the lunch. I heard you stopped by her gallery yesterday. That was so nice of you, and she was delighted to see you. She told you what happened, right?" he asked, dropping his voice to a whisper even though it was only the two of them. He mimed touching his neck.

"Yes. She did," she said, feigning horror at the prospect of Isla's diamond being stolen. "Who took it? Do you have any idea?"

He shook his head, and the corners of his mouth curved down. "It's terrible. That was an engagement diamond, too. It saddens me," he said, bringing a hand to his heart. "I've been on nonstop calls with the insurance company since it happened. You wouldn't believe the amount of paperwork they require for stolen goods."

"You reported it to them already?"

"Of course," he said, dropping his hand to the leather in a slap for emphasis. "You can't let thieves get away with anything."

"No, you can't. You definitely can't," she said emphatically, seconding him. They agreed on that count because she had no intention of letting the thieves get away with snagging her diamond. She didn't want Eli taking the fall, either, if it turned out—oh God, she hoped it turned out this way—that he wasn't the one who'd stolen the money, that someone had set him up, maybe even his own fiancée. But if he had bamboozled the funds, she would try once more to convince him to do the right thing—to return the money to her mother and his company without getting the authorities involved. She just needed the damn diamonds in her hand in order to get him to listen. Otherwise, he'd deny, deny, deny that he had them. "Are you going to get her a new one when the insurance pays out?"

He shook his head, a look of pride spreading to his blue eyes. "Nope. And that's how I'm not going to let the bad guys get away with the crime of stealing a beautiful gift of love. I'm turning the other cheek," he said, then demonstrated by raising his chin high and shifting his gaze.

"But how are you letting it go if you're pursuing the insurance money?" she asked, pointing out the flaw in his logic.

He held his index finger in the air, stabbing it to make a point. "I've decided when the insurance payout comes, I'm not even going to buy a replacement. I'm going to donate the payout to our favorite charity in Africa."

There it was again. The charity mention. He seemed damn proud of it. How could a man so focused on giving money away have stolen it for personal gain? Isla had to be the perpetrator. She'd probably Svengali'd him with her charity-this and charity-that routine. Maybe he didn't even know she'd taken all those stones and squirreled them away. "The charity that helps support schools for kids affected by the former diamond economy?"

"Yes!" he said, his eyes lighting up. "I think it's the perfect solution to a terrible crime. We don't technically need another diamond, after all. I have plenty, and you have yours, and I trust it's safe and—"

At eleven thirty on the dot, his office phone bleated loudly.

Thank God.

She hoped that was for her.

Eli didn't even acknowledge the call. Good. She wanted the staff at the club to answer it. Twenty seconds later, Clarissa rapped gently. "Knock knock," she said. "I have a phone call for Steph. It's Tommy."

Steph jerked her head to the side. Adopted a look of utter surprise. "Why isn't he calling me on my cell . . . ," she said, then dipped her hand into her purse and fished around, as if hunting for the phone.

But she hadn't brought it. So that she could pull off this ruse.

"He sounds sad," Clarissa added in a whisper.

Steph wanted to punch her fist in the air. Tommy was supposed to sound sad. Poor Tommy and his heartbreak. She turned to her stepfather. "I forgot my cell. Is there any chance I could just . . ." She let her voice trail off. If he offered on his own, it would be all the better.

Eli rose and gestured grandly. "Of course. Use my office. As long as you need. Let me know when you're done."

"Just hit line nine," Clarissa added, tipping her chin toward the desk.

Steph laced her fingers together and thanked them both. As if on cue, Clarissa exited with Eli right behind her. He shut the door. When it clicked, she raced over to lock it, then marched to the desk and picked up line nine.

"Hello?"

Sobs greeted her. "I'm so sad. I'm all alone with the snorkel gear and can you please talk to me?"

"Of course, Tommy," she said to Jake, and a smile burst on her face. She was alone in Eli's office with the artwork. She shucked off those brief flashes of guilt. There was no room for guilt, no space for second thoughts. She was within reach of solving the mystery.

She was going to be the one to open that frame, snag the jewels, and return them to their rightful owners. She would see that justice was done. For everyone. The investors who'd lost millions in retirement money would get it back, her mom would see the return of some of her seed money, and she might very well save Eli from further trouble.

But they weren't the only ones.

She was also doing this for Jake. He was the most dedicated man she knew, and she admired his drive to support his family. Finding the diamonds and returning them to the fund would help him finish the job.

"Just dab your eyes and I'll be right back," she said to her partner in Robin Hooding.

"I will. I've got my Hello Kitty tissues," he said with a wailing cry that nearly made her crack up.

She set the receiver on the desk, raced to the wall, stood on the couch, and grabbed the edge of the frame. Thank the Lord it wasn't a huge frame—maybe a foot and a half on each side. Gingerly, she lifted it off the hook. She shook the frame, and something in it rattled.

Her heart sailed into the stratosphere.

Excitement roared through her.

All the clues had added up. All the dead ends were in the rearview mirror now. All the strikeouts were becoming home runs. A grand slam, even, judging from the zipping sounds the gems made as she held the frame.

A focused thrill pinged through her body. Setting the frame on the couch, she flipped it around and surveyed the back side. Perfect. It was covered in sturdy brown paper that was stapled on, as most framed art was. Steph dug around in her bag and grabbed a pocketknife Jake had given her to use. Flipping open the blade, she carefully sliced a thin line a few inches along the bottom corner, then up the adjacent side. She peeled the paper and held her breath.

She peered into the opening, and her heart nearly rocketed to the moon. There it was. A slim, plastic black cylinder. Like the size of a travel toothbrush container. It was taped to the inside of the frame.

Wow, she mouthed.

This moment was truly surreal. Steph Anderson, adventure tour operator and marine biologist, was transforming into a treasure hunter—a modern-day Robin Hood.

Dipping her fingers into the paper opening, she undid the tape and slid out the tube. The hair on her arms stood on end as she raised it in front of her face. She opened the cap and tipped it into her palm. The diamonds bumped and rattled as they slid along the chute of the plastic tube where they'd been hiding. On a mad dash for her hand. In less than a second, she'd have a handful of precious gems.

They landed in her palm.

A whole handful of . . . nuts.

CHAPTER FIFTEEN

"Tell me everything you learned."

Jake parked himself on a bench at the edge of Seven Mile Beach, grinding his jaw. If he was this stewed over nuts, he couldn't even imagine how frustrated Steph must be sitting through a lunch with her stepfather.

No wonder Ferdinand had been crunching on cashews when Jake spotted him leaving Eli's office. The question was—had Ferdinand planted the nuts, or had he been roadblocked by them, too? Maybe he'd been hunting for diamonds and came up with nuts. Or maybe Ferdinand was in on the trick and had planted the nuts in the frame on behalf of Eli.

That was the problem. Ferdinand was a wild card. He might be working for Eli, or he might be working against Eli.

Jake hoped Kate's intel would help him figure out which side the man was on.

Kate began her debrief. "Ferdinand Costello has worked in the nightclub business for eight years. He managed the facility for its prior owner before Eli bought it. Eli kept him on board to run the place," Kate said, sharing details she'd gleaned. "He helped with the renovation, helped with the hiring, helped line up security."

"Is he local?"

"Yes. Born and raised in the Islands. He has a *huge* family. Like five brothers and two sisters big."

Jake whistled in admiration for the size. "That is big, and that's also pretty much the definition of motivation. That is, if he supports them. Do we know?"

"Seems to be the case. His dad died a few years ago of cancer," Kate said, and Jake's heart ached for the guy.

"Sorry to hear," he said softly.

"Yeah, me, too," Kate said, though Jake couldn't help but wonder if the pressure to support his family now was making Ferdinand take a walk on the dark side. Ferdinand might very well have played the role of Mr. Smith, diamond thief.

"What about that tattoo? Anything to it?"

"Apparently, he has a few pet snakes," Kate said.

Jake's stomach curled at the thought. He tended to agree with Indiana Jones on this count. *Snakes. Why did it have to be snakes?* "What about Tristan O'Doole?" he asked, moving on. "Tell me about the restaurant guy."

"Ah, Tristan. He's from Boston. Been around for a long time and has lived in the Caymans for twenty years. He had a few restaurants in the Boston area a while ago. One was a big success initially, but then it turned out the place was swimming in debt. He started Tristan's fifteen years ago and it's become a mildly successful place on the island. I checked out a few restaurant trade magazines from years ago, though, and it looks like one of the reasons his first restaurant went belly-up was he'd tried to make custom coffee and liquor drinks. He started investing in manufacturing a whole line of coffee and whiskey," Kate said, with an *isn't-that-odd* tone. "I mean, I get that some people put whiskey in their coffee, but it hardly seems like something one intentionally needs to mix and market."

Jake nodded and stroked his chin, an idea forming. "He's trying to do business with Eli. I wonder if he's aiming to resurrect some sort of idea like that," he mused.

"Apparently, he's tried his hand at specialty drinks a few times with limited success. Looks like he's worked up a few concoctions over the years and has tried to use his restaurants as launching pads for new drinks and whatnot. Most have fizzled. A year ago he tried out some strange chocolate drinks at Tristan's that didn't quite win any fans."

"Interesting. Since Eli's investment that went belly-up was in cocoa beans. Maybe he should have done a deal for Eli's chocolate because the ones I tried from his secret stash were damn good," Jake said, making a mental note to ask Steph what she could find out about Tristan. "How is the restaurant here doing? Any debt trouble?"

"None that I could find. Seems solid enough. Looks like he hit his stride with this one," she said.

"OK, so the money troubles are behind him, making him less suspicious."

He leaned forward, resting a palm on his thigh, staring out at the vast expanse of blue. Some kiteboarders skimmed the small waves near the shore, and off in the distance, a pair of jet skiers cut clean lines through the water. Farther toward the horizon, fishing boats bobbed in the water. "What about International Diamonds? Were you able to find an employee named Monica?"

"I called International Diamonds and was able to get her last name. Monica Smith," Kate said, and Jake sat up straight on the bench, like his spine had become a ruler.

"That was the name used at the front desk of Steph's hotel," he said, then quickly explained about the man who'd arrived at her hotel claiming a meeting.

"Right," Kate said calmly, her tone a counter to Jake's enthusiasm at putting clues together. As if she were trying to temper him. "But that's kind of a common fake last name, Jake."

"I know," he said with a heavy sigh. "Still, what are the chances it would be used by both the guy at the hotel and this woman?"

"Um, pretty good?"

He scoffed. "Anyway, did you find anything on her?"

"Nope. Zero. Zilch. Nada. I scoured the usual sources. I wasn't able to track down a Monica Smith living in the Caymans."

Maybe Kate thought it was merely a coincidence that she shared the same last name as the man who dubbed himself Mr. Smith. But Jake didn't. The woman had been following him earlier. She'd been suspicious of him days ago. She knew he had a blue-tinted diamond worth ten grand, and she'd been skulking around the bar at the beach the night he was with Steph.

Wait.

He straightened his spine. How had he missed it? He smacked his palm against his forehead. Just last night Steph had been telling him about a woman who looked familiar. A woman she'd seen at Isla's party. Monica was turning diamonds; Isla was involved with a man who'd stolen diamonds, and Jake Fucking Harlowe had been so into his partner last night he hadn't bothered to follow through on her tip.

The buck stopped here.

No more slip-ups. No more missteps. Today's narrow focus on work was all he could afford. Every tip, every instinct had to be examined. He couldn't afford to lose his edge.

But he had it back.

Because just like he sensed danger, just like he knew how to find the stolen Strad, he was sure that Monica was onto them. Most likely, she was working with a partner—a man who'd ambled over to the front desk posing as Mr. Smith.

Monica and Ferdinand?

Monica and Tristan?

He wasn't sure who her Mr. Smith was. But he was dead sure Monica was working with him.

CHAPTER SIXTEEN

Salty peanuts.

Honey.

Almonds.

She seethed, detesting them all. Because they sure seemed to prove that something was fishy.

"I'll have the Asian chicken salad," she said to the waiter at Tristan's, fixing on a phony smile. "Please hold the *peanuts*."

"And the Cobb salad for me," Eli added with a smile.

Her stepfather had no clue she'd had the nuts in her hand. After cursing silently to the moon and back, she'd dropped them into the plastic tube with a *plink, plink, plink*. Then tucked the tube in place behind the frame, taped it down, and secured the brown paper in place. She'd washed her hands, erasing the traces of nuts.

Sure, if Eli removed the frame from the wall, he might notice someone had been poking around in the paper, but she didn't care anymore. She hadn't stolen anything. Nothing could happen to her, and there were enough people after his jewels that she didn't think any fingers would point to her as the culprit.

Culprit of what? Of checking out a tube of nuts nestled inside a picture frame? She was no law-enforcement expert, but that hardly seemed a crime. Besides, she had half a mind to throw in the towel at this point. Eli was too smart, too clever, and too damn determined to win. Obviously, he knew someone was after his diamonds. Why else would he put freaking nuts in a frame? Just for kicks? Or as a taunt? She was willing to bet he'd hidden nuts there as a decoy. He'd probably purposely planted clues all over town as to the fake location of the diamonds.

While she didn't think he was trying to fool her, per se, he was certainly trying to fool everyone else by dropping hints that he had diamonds in the frames of his art.

She scoffed to herself.

That was part of his plan. Throw everyone off the scent with false clues. But just to toy with them, he hid worthless nuts in the frame instead. Turning it into a gag gift. He was one step ahead of everyone. He always had been. He tricked, and then he tricked back, like he'd done with her mom when he'd fooled around. Today she'd been the one to sit on the whoopee cushion.

Now it was lunchtime, and this was supposedly why she'd arrived early—to dine with him. She tried desperately to shove aside her frustration. After they ordered, she asked how business was at Sapphire, biting back her lingering anger over how he'd funded the club—with her mother's money. But still, Sapphire was an easier topic of conversation than *where are your damn diamonds?*

Business was great, he said.

Of course.

She inquired about Isla's gallery.

Everything was fantastic there, he told her.

Naturally.

"And are you able to expand it like you wanted? Isla mentioned something about annexing the shop next door?"

He downed some of his champagne, then nodded enthusiastically. "Yes, as a matter of fact I just got word before you came in. The deal is on, and I called Isla to share the good news while you were on the phone with your friend."

Ah, so that's what the deal was that would *thrill* her. No surprise there. Once again, Eli was getting everything he wanted. The woman, the art, the jewels, the club, the goddamn never-ending string of unbroken luck.

She clenched her fists as he spoke. But after listening to him go on and on about how the sky rained gold coins and rainbows in the wonderful old Land of Eli, she couldn't take it. She was getting nowhere with her private-eye act, and being in his pocket had done little to help her pull off the reverse jewel heist.

Time for an entirely new tactic.

Honesty.

"Eli," she said, snapping her napkin from the table and spreading it in her lap.

"Yes, my dear?"

"There's something I want to talk to you about," she began, and was ready to dive into questions about his hedge fund. She hadn't scripted this moment, but she didn't need to. Because she was going to speak from the heart and ask point-blank if he'd skimmed money off the top. She was done dancing around the topic. She was finished with deciphering clues. She didn't have the damn diamonds to make her point, but she had words.

He held up a hand, like a stop sign. "No, my dear. I need to talk to you. I've been thinking about what you said the other day at brunch."

"You have?" she asked, taken aback.

"Indeed. I've done some soul searching and you're right. I wasn't fair to Shelly."

Her chin clanged to the ground like a cartoon character. Eli didn't apologize for anything. This was front-page news. "In the divorce? You weren't fair in the divorce you mean?" she asked, needing to be very specific. She didn't want an ounce of confusion about this moment.

He shrugged an admission as he lifted his champagne flute. "That. Yes. But also while I was married to her. I wasn't fair then, either."

"What?" She rubbed her finger against her ear. Was she hearing things?

He sighed heavily. "Look. I've made some mistakes. I was, for lack of a better word, a bit of a schmuck."

"A bit?" Her voice rose. To the ceiling. Perhaps to Mars, even.

"OK, more than a bit," he conceded as a waiter brought gourmet burgers to a nearby table. "I could have done many things differently. Isla has been helping me to see that. She's helping me to be a better man. To make up for my past mistakes and to move on with a clean slate."

"So, like, making up for cheating on Mom multiple times?" Steph countered.

"Now, Steph, my dear," he said in a firm voice, setting down the glass.

But before he could continue, the salt-and-pepper-haired Tristan scurried over, beaming as he reached the table. He dropped a hand on Eli's shoulder. "How is everything so far? Is my waitstaff treating you well?"

"They're the best on the island, Tristan. Always have been," Eli said, flashing his trademark smile.

"Ah, you flatter me, but I'll take it." Tristan wagged a finger at Eli. "I'll be sure to send you one of my new chocolate concoctions for dessert," he said, then gestured to the maître d' stand before Eli could reply. "Must go."

"Chocolate concoctions?" Steph asked.

"He fancies himself a chocolatier," Eli said dismissively.

"There are far worse things to be."

He flashed a grin. "So true."

With Tristan out of sight, Steph returned to the conversation, "Are you going to apologize to Mom now? Maybe try to settle matters a bit more fairly?"

"Let's not get into those matters. I said I was sorry, and I fully intend to let Shelly know that I'm working hard on becoming a better man and turning over a new leaf. And I will do everything I can to see if I can make things more equitable."

Steph raised an eyebrow and shot an approving nod. "Like paying alimony? Changing the terms of the settlement?"

He nodded, but then made a rolling gesture with his hands. "Let's not spend our time delving into the specifics of dirty little money matters. Suffice it to say, I'm making changes, and Isla is by my side every step of the way. Some of the money from the sale of the Lynx art has gone to charity," he said, and though she'd previously wondered if Isla was somehow laundering diamond money through the charity, the thought now occurred to her that his new giving side might truly be part of this makeover. The possibility tugged at her heart. "We're hosting a small gathering at her gallery in a few days to raise more money for the African charity. You should come to it if you're still in town."

"I'll try."

"This is all part of my commitment to reinvention," he said, gesturing to himself, as if he were presenting the new mold of stepdad.

She thoroughly approved of Eli 2.0.

"You're trying to become a new man," she said, wonder coloring her tone. A happy, contented sensation bloomed inside her chest. All along, everyone had thought he was irredeemable. Her mom, Andrew, Jake—they were steadfast that Eli was all bad. But this was why she came to the Caymans early. This was her hope. That he was changing. That he was willing to move beyond his mistakes. It bolstered her to take another step. To try harder to be the one to help him make amends. "Does this whole coming clean approach extend to your company?"

He cocked his head to the side. "What do you mean?"

"Eli," she said in a soft but chiding tone as she went out on a limb here. She glanced from left to right, leaned in closer, and lowered her voice. "I'm twenty-eight. I'm active online. I hear what people say about your company and why you left."

She'd heard no such thing online, but it seemed a plausible enough thing to read about, and perhaps it would help her get to the truth.

"What did you hear?"

Her voice dipped even lower. "They say you, ya know"—she made a motion with her hands, like she was sweeping—"skimmed a little off the top."

His eyebrows shot into his hairline. "They say that?" He sounded incredulous. "Oh, ho ho. They say wrong. Why do you think I left the Eli Fund? I loved that company, but I could not tolerate Andrew's chicanery any longer."

Now it was her turn to furrow her brow. "Andrew? What do you mean?"

He beckoned for her to come closer, and she practically rested her torso across the plates and silverware because she was dying to hear this new spin.

"He stole money from the shareholders," Eli whispered, and if a person could be comprised solely of one emotion, one feeling, one sensation, it had happened to Steph. She was stitched through with shock. In seconds, her mind began to spin with new twists and turns. *Was Andrew setting up Jake? Was Andrew setting me up? He'd always seemed like a good guy, but was he the one who'd stolen the money? Had he tried to pin the stolen funds on Eli? What if Andrew had taken the money? What if the diamonds were just Eli's diamonds, and Andrew's evidence was doctored?*

Her stomach rose and fell like a roller coaster.

"He did?" she asked, her throat dry.

Eli nodded. "That's what I believe to be true."

"Why do you believe that? Why would he do that?"

"He wanted to impress your mother."

"Why?"

Eli shot her a look that said, *You can't be serious*. "Steph. You really don't know?"

She shook her head.

"Andrew has been in love with her forever. He's known her since college. They're old friends. But he wants to be more. So what does he do when she's single? He nicks a little off the top because he thinks he can buy her love."

"You're saying he skimmed money off the company to impress my mom?"

"I'm saying that *if* there was money missing from the Eli Fund, fingers should be pointed at him, not at yours truly. That's all," he said, then shook his head in disbelief. "And I highly suspect it's to feed this lifelong obsession he's had with Shelly. He thought he would be the one to comfort her after your father died."

She winced. She didn't like hearing anyone talk this way about her father. "Please don't bring my dad into this," she whispered, her voice threatening to break.

"I'm sorry, dear. But you asked why I believed that. And the reality is Andrew has been carrying a torch for Shelly for years."

Steph cringed. "But he's married and has children," she said, but then again, so was Eli when he dipped his stick elsewhere.

He nodded. "Indeed. All the more reason, as you can see, why I don't trust the man. All the more reason why I got out of that company."

After the waiter set down the salads, Eli dug into his and pronounced it delicious. "I could eat salad every day and be happy," he said with a broad smile. "And I used to just be a steak man."

A memory resurfaced of dinners growing up, and Eli manning the barbecue. He loved grilling; he'd hated salads. But he'd changed, evidently. Fine. That was over something seemingly small, like one's regular choice of meat or veggies for lunch. But he was changing in other ways, too, like giving more money to charity. Was it possible that he'd seen the light? That his love for Isla and vice versa had transformed him?

Their affection for each other seemed truly genuine. Maybe love could change a cad, a thief, a bastard. Maybe there were no stolen diamonds to retrieve. Only diamonds he well and truly owned.

Steph ate her chicken salad, wondering whether her stepfather's personal makeover changed her next steps.

When the chocolate dessert concoction arrived, Eli seemed to savor the first sip. Then he wrinkled his nose. "Nuts," he said in disgust.

"There are nuts in it?"

"I hate nuts," he said.

"Funny," she said drily. "We have that in common."

❧

Sometime during lunch, the sky heated up. The blissful island air turned hot, as her weather app had predicted, and the sun sweltered. Steph tugged at the cotton of her sundress as she walked to Eli's car.

"Every now and then we get these brief heat waves," he said with a shrug as he opened the door for her. She slid inside, and when he joined her, he cranked up the air-conditioning. The cool jets were welcome, and Steph sighed in appreciation.

"Best car AC ever," she said.

Eli patted the dashboard. "It is. It's like the perfect blast of chilly air, but never too much."

"Sure beats the crummy AC in my rental," she said as she relaxed in the beige leather seat as they drove toward the club.

"What did you rent?"

"A Jeep."

At the light, he slowed, then turned to her. "Take this one."

"What?"

"Yes. Take it. I have another car. Use this while you're here."

"Eli, I can't do that."

"You just said the AC isn't working well."

"It's not, but—"

"And this AC works swimmingly, right?"

"Yes," she muttered.

"So drive it while you're here. There's absolutely no reason not to," he said as the light changed and they cruised along the strip of concrete, the ocean hugging them on one side.

"You don't have to do that."

"I know I don't have to. But I want to," he said, patting her thigh in a fatherly way. "Look, I know I wasn't a model husband, or even always a good man, when you were younger. But I've always thought of you as my daughter, and I've always liked the idea of helping you. Maybe I haven't done enough to make that clear over the past few years, but I'm trying to be more giving now. To stop being so focused on Eli Thompson and to focus more on others. And if something as small as letting you use my car for the next few days helps you, then it would mean the world to me if you said yes."

The heat of the sun warmed her shoulder through the closed window, and the vents piped cool air. There was no point saying no, especially if this was part of the amends. She said yes. When they reached the club, Eli parked the car out front and told her he'd be right back. "Just need to grab my extra keys from my desk drawer for you," he said.

"Thank you again."

She got out of the car and leaned against the passenger door as she waited for him. The security guy was there, like a sentry. He nodded at her, a flicker of a smile at the corners of his lips. She flashed back to something Isla had said at her house party.

"Oh, Eli got called away into the club. Had to check on a security issue there. You can never be too careful, you know."

As the man guarded the door like he was the last line of defense in a war, Steph wondered what sort of security matters the club had faced a few nights ago. Come to think of it, the evening Eli was called away happened to be precisely one night after Jake and Steph had scoped out the club—during that stakeout, Jake had spotted the manager eating nuts while leaving Eli's office.

Her spine tingled.

Ferdinand had been at Isla's party. He'd been at Happy Turtle during one of her visits. Had he also slipped into Steph's hotel room?

She wrapped her arms around herself even though she wasn't cold. A minute later, the security guy opened the door for Eli. He wasn't alone. The inked man joined him. Steph tensed, moving away from the car.

"Steph, I want you to meet Ferdinand Costello. He manages this club like a pro," Eli said and clapped him on the back. "He was out running some errands for me, but now he's back."

Ferdinand shot her a closed-mouth smile and offered a hand to shake. She took it, nerves storming through her as she searched his brown eyes for any sort of clue that he might be Mr. Smith.

"Good to meet you," he said, clasping her hand longer than needed. "We've all heard so much about you. You're the adventure tour superstar."

"She is indeed," Eli said, stepping next to her to squeeze a shoulder.

"What are your favorite spots? Eden Rock? Stingray City? Happy Turtle Cove?"

The little hairs on her arms stood on end. Happy Turtle was the combination to her safe.

CHAPTER SEVENTEEN

Two could play at this game.

Oh, yes, they could.

Jake left the beach in a huff. Because Jake did the spying. Jake did the investigating.

He did not like it one bit when someone tried to turn the tables. That woman was not going to beat him. On his return to the diamond district, he rang International Diamonds.

"Hey, I'm calling to see if Monica Smith will be working this afternoon."

"She'll be here. Shall I give her a message?" the woman on the other end of the phone asked.

"Nope. I have a new stone and I need her keen eye. I'll just head over shortly with the rock."

"Wonderful. We look forward to it."

He laid in wait outside International Diamonds. Nothing broke his focus. He kept watch at the end of the block. He sat at a café across the street with a view of the shop, eyes on the door the whole time. But Monica never showed up. She didn't return to the store. She didn't return to Tristan's, either. She was nowhere to be seen. He waited, and waited, and waited, and finally had to call it a day. At least he'd been relentless. He'd been on his game, even if the game hadn't been on.

When he returned to the hotel, Steph was pulling into the parking lot in Eli's gleaming black Audi.

"Nice new wheels," he said, arching an eyebrow in question, and she told him her stepdad had given her the car. But her voice was flat, a note of sadness to it.

He'd seen her mad, he'd seen her happy, he'd seen her feisty. But he'd never witnessed listlessness from Steph Anderson. Energy and passion had always unfurled from her.

Until now.

He gripped her shoulders and dropped a quick kiss on her lips. Work had ruled the day, and now it was time to help her. "You need a piña colada and you need it stat."

⁓

A hammock hung between two palm trees at the edge of the hotel pool, beckoning. The branches of the tree canopied it, shading out the harsher rays of the afternoon sun. The waves gently dusted the shore, and the splash of teenagers in the hotel pool crackled in the background.

"This hammock has your name written all over it," he said, holding a drink in each hand. Ordinarily, he wouldn't touch a froufrou drink with a ten-foot pole, but when in Rome . . .

Or more likely, when your woman is in a funk, sometimes you have to go for the full tropical-drink treatment, complete with red paper umbrellas and swirly straws in each cup.

Steph flopped onto the crisscross ropes of the hammock and made a clawing gesture with one hand. "Drink. Now. Please."

"One fruity, over-the-top drink at your service. The best medicine I've ever known for a crappy day," he said, handing her the drink.

She took a long, thirsty gulp.

"Careful of the brain freeze," he said as he joined her on the hammock so they were facing each other.

"I honestly wouldn't mind my brain being frozen right now. Then I could stop thinking."

"Talk to me. Tell me what happened. I know you're bummed about the nuts," he said.

"At first it was the nuts," she said with a scoff that turned into a deep, incredulous laugh. "It felt like I'd gotten a pie in my face at a carnival. But then he told me at lunch about how he's trying to change, and he's trying to do right by my mom and make up for how unfair he was in the divorce," she said, her voice softening. "And that's honestly all I wanted in the first place. I didn't come here hunting diamonds. I came here early for a personal family reason."

Jake nodded slowly, taking his time to process. As her lover, he wanted to be supportive and respectful of the family matters, even if they didn't see eye to eye. But as her partner in un-crime, he wanted her by his side.

"I get it. You feel torn," he said, keeping his response simple and straight down the middle. He knocked back more of his beverage, brain freeze risks be damned. Stretching his arm to the grass, he set his drink on the grass under the hammock and reached for her leg. He rubbed her calf, enjoying the warmth of her skin. Then he focused his words on the greater good. "I know you feel pulled, and I know you're frustrated, too, that we're coming up empty. But we're close, so close. And I know we can set things right. The diamonds are somewhere here on this island."

She shot him a helpless stare. "The diamonds could be anywhere. *Anywhere*. That's the problem. We've turned over every possible stone, and they've come up empty," she said, then under her breath she added, "and maybe they should. Maybe we should leave well enough alone."

"I'm not ready to give up," he said, trying to stay upbeat for the both of them. He had the big carrot of Andrew's incentive dangling in front of him, but that wasn't the only reason he wanted to soldier on.

He didn't believe in giving up. He wasn't ready to throw in the towel. Sure, some cases went cold, but this one felt crackable, and he didn't want to lose his partner.

"What if he didn't even take the money from his company? What if someone else is the Bernie Madoff in this situation? What if it's Andrew?" she asked, her voice thready with doubt as she shared something Eli had said to her at lunch. Seemed her stepdad was trying to cast blame back on his former business partner, and nothing could be more suspicious than that, in Jake's mind. "And then he told me that Andrew has been in love with my mother for years," Steph added with a *what's-the-deal-with-that* look.

"He said that?" Jake furrowed his brow.

She wrapped her lips around the red straw and drank. "Yes. It seems like a strange thing to say out of nowhere, doesn't it?"

Jake sighed and slid his palm down his face. "Actually, it's not completely random. When I talked to Andrew on the phone yesterday, he mentioned out of the blue how pretty your mom is."

Steph crinkled her freckled nose, then set her drink on the ground. "Really? Ugh. That just kind of grosses me out right now."

"I have to admit, I thought it was a little odd to mention it. Not that your mom isn't gorgeous, because," he said, stopping to gesture to the evidence in front of him in the form of the woman's beautiful daughter, "obviously she produced you, but it was strange to say."

"Jake," she said softly, pushing up on her elbows. "Do you trust Andrew? How do we know for sure what he's told you is legit?"

"Kate vetted everything beforehand. I wouldn't have taken the job if I didn't believe his info was solid and checked out," he said, squeezing her calf for emphasis and putting his drink down, too.

"What if Kate made a mistake, though?"

He blinked, looking at her like she was crazy. "Excuse me?"

"What if your sister missed something? What if those documents and e-mails were doctored?"

He shook his head, his jaw set hard. "No. I saw them myself, and besides, Kate specializes in document analysis. She doesn't make mistakes," he said, his tone firm.

"But everyone makes mistakes," she said softly.

He cocked his head to the side, not liking this new direction. "Then by that rule of thumb, what if you made a mistake? What if you were wrong?"

"What are you saying I'm wrong about?"

"I'm saying you're wrong in stating that the evidence is false. I think maybe," he said, taking his time with the next words, "you're letting these gifts he gives you sway you from the truth."

"What gifts?"

"The car," he said matter-of-factly. "He gave you his car to use. No wonder you're believing the lie he served up about Andrew."

Her eyes blazed with anger, but her voice was menacingly quiet when she spoke. "I don't care about material things. I don't care about the car. I care about my family. OK? I'm just like you, only *excuse me* that we're not above reproach. I get that Eli isn't perfect. I know that as well as anyone. He's made a ton of mistakes and he's hurt people. But he's the only father I've ever had, and even if he's less than perfect, I would hope you of all people would understand the ties that bind," she said, sitting up straight, anger radiating off her.

Shit.

He was hitting below the belt, and it wasn't fair. He couldn't even pretend to know how torn she must feel. "Steph," he said softly, running his fingertips down her arm. She shirked away. "I'm sorry I said that. I do understand the pull. I just don't want you to be blind to what's going on," he said, then tried once more to touch her. Selfishly, he couldn't risk fighting with her like this. There was too much at stake, and he couldn't jeopardize the case just because he disagreed with her. She might tip off Eli. She might turn her back on him. She might cross him.

But he also hated to see her hurting.

He ran his fingers down her bare skin once more. This time, she let him. "I know it's hard," he whispered.

"It is hard. It's really fucking hard," she said in a broken whisper, devoid of anger now, laced only with sadness.

That he knew. That he understood. And that he could comfort as a man who cared deeply for a woman. He wrapped his arms around her and pulled her close, petting her hair. "I know, Steph. I know. And I know how important family is. Trust me, I do."

Trust.

That's what this all came down to. He still wasn't entirely sure if they trusted each other, but she fit so damn well in his arms that it was almost impossible to fathom that they might still doubt each other.

She pulled away a few inches. "And on top of all of that stuff in here," she said, tapping her heart, "I feel like we're being set up. Everywhere I turn, we hit a snag."

"That's the nature of a case like this. Three steps forward. Two steps back."

"I wouldn't be surprised if the diamonds are in Africa at this point with the charity. Or with Ferdinand. He made the strangest comment when I left today that made me think he knew the combo to my safe. Or maybe Tristan has them. He's trying to do a deal with my stepdad to carry some new drink."

"Or with the diamond saleswoman," he said, then described Monica to her, down to the details of her glasses.

Steph's big blue eyes blinked. "Are you kidding me?"

"No. I'm not," he said, tilting his head to the side. "Why do you sound so surprised?"

"Because that woman was at Isla's house party. She sounds exactly like the same Monica."

"Holy shit," he said, the wind knocked out of him in surprise. "It's got to be her. She has to be the one who took your diamond. She was the one who told me the value of it when I went to International

Diamonds with you. I bet she followed us that day. Remember, we heard a car peeling out in the garage where I . . ." He let his voice trail off to remind her of their afternoon in the back of her Jeep.

She rolled her eyes playfully, and that one light gesture from her in the midst of her frustration hooked into his heart. He wanted to be the one to lift her up, to whisk her away from a crappy day. "Yes, I remember. Anyway, you think she was following us?"

"It's entirely possible that she wanted that diamond of yours from the second I showed it to her at the store. She could have followed us to figure out where you were staying."

"See? This is my point. I'm being followed. People are stealing from me. My stepdad's manager makes odd comments. I just want to do my job. But there's still this one big, fat issue for me," she said, stopping to take a beat and meeting his gaze. "What if Eli is telling me the truth?"

"Do you believe him?"

"I don't know what to believe. It's not even about the jewels anymore, Jake. Or who they should or shouldn't belong to," she said, dragging a hand through her hair. "I don't know what to believe about him."

He didn't know how to reassure her or if he even could. He didn't have to grapple with the same issues. Eli had helped raise her, he'd lived with her, he'd taken her to kiss stingrays. That bond wasn't easily dismissed, despite his sins and omissions on other fronts.

But to Jake, Eli was simply the target. He didn't have to divorce his emotions; there were none.

He ran his hands down her legs, reaching for her foot. Her eyes drifted closed, and she moaned softly as he pressed his thumbs against the ball of her foot. A contented sigh fell from her lips as he massaged her heels, her arch, her toes, all the way to her little pinkie. He wiggled it. She laughed, a sweet sound, like bells.

He rubbed his way up, digging his fingers into the strong muscles of her legs. Her legs had hooked him that first night. They were one of the things he noticed about her in the bar. How strong and athletic she was, making her his type physically. But in the last week he'd learned she was much more than that. What started as physical had morphed into something more. Into the kind of something where he wanted her to be happy, where he wanted to bring that sparkle back to her eyes.

He reached her thighs, and she let one knee fall to the side.

Oh hell. He wasn't strong enough. He didn't possess enough restraint to rub her legs in a hammock in public. He wanted her too much.

He reached for her hand and took her to their room.

Once inside, he lifted her dress over her shoulders, then slid off her panties. She took off his clothes. They didn't say anything. Only sighs. Only murmurs. Only touches. Words weren't needed. He wanted to comfort her with his touch.

Walking backward to the bed, he pulled her on top of him. He cupped her cheeks in his hands, brushing her hair from her face, stopping to look at her—to memorize her face, to run his thumb along her jaw.

Her lips parted, and there it was. That hazy, sexy, vulnerable look that he adored seeing. One of yearning, one of longing.

She whispered his name. "Take me. I want you to take me."

"I want to have you," he said, his voice low and needy. He was desperate for her. "God, I want to have you."

He reached for a condom on the nightstand, but before he could put it on, she grasped the packet, opened it, and rolled it on him. He twitched in her palm, loving, just fucking loving her touch. Lust and desire swelled inside him as she lowered herself. All the air in his lungs rushed out as her heat gripped him.

She dropped her hands to his chest, her palms pressing hard as she rolled her hips against him.

Again and again.

Over and over.

It felt so damn good. This closeness. This connection. This moment with this woman. All the moments with her. Currents of pleasure surged inside him as she circled her hips.

"*This,*" she said on a murmur. "This is my favorite part."

He knew what she meant. She didn't mean the position or this particular second in their love-making. He knew she meant the two of them, and all that they'd shared.

"You," she said. "You're my favorite part."

He grabbed her waist. Stared in her eyes as she rode him. "You're mine, too," he said, his voice dry and husky. "I swear you're mine, too."

She moaned, a throaty, sexy sound that somehow made him crave her even more. He wanted to be buried deep inside her. To do this again and again, over and over, every goddamn night. The heat inside him spread, turning to wildfire. Because of her—her beautiful body, her gorgeous face, and her amazing heart.

He grasped her hips and flipped her over onto her back. "Need to have you. Need to take you hard now," he said, parting her legs wider, hooking them up on his shoulders. He had her pinned. At his mercy.

"I need it, too."

He drove into her. She threw her head back, her long neck exposed, her blonde hair spread across the pillow, and her legs on his shoulders. Her mouth fell open, her pants grew heavier, and she was nearing the edge. "Don't wait." She moaned. "Don't wait this time. Just come with me."

She'd read his mind. So much for his promise to give her three before his one. He couldn't hold back if he tried. In seconds, she was trembling in bliss as his own shudders racked through him.

He collapsed on her, folding her in his arms, not wanting to let go. She snuggled up against him, and he held her tighter.

"I meant it. You're my favorite part of this trip," she said.

"And you're mine," he said.

He was so tempted to ask what would happen when the trip was over and they returned to Florida. Neither one had voiced it. Neither had acknowledged that they didn't live that far from each other. Maybe now was the time to do that. A relationship was a scary beast, but maybe they could find a way to try.

She pushed her rear against him, cuddling closer, wrapping his arm tightly to her chest. "I kind of don't care about the diamonds anymore," she murmured.

He tensed briefly, then tried to let the tightness in his muscles fade. But it was hard. Because he still cared. That was the issue. The more he got lost in her, the more he risked what he loved most. Even if he was dangerously close to feeling something that he hadn't dared experience in ages.

She could come and go from the gig. She was free to walk away. He didn't have the same luxury.

CHAPTER EIGHTEEN

The music drowned out all other sounds. It pounded in his ears and thrummed in his veins. Loud, obnoxious, and far too techno for his taste. Tonight was hip-hop remix night at Sapphire, and Jake could do without the reverb. But he was determined to tail Monica.

She was here at Sapphire. On the second-floor balcony. Surveying the scene. Perusing it from behind those black cat's-eye glasses. A part of him wondered who was following whom. She or him. Because he was tailing her, and she was onto him, and they were circling each other like gunslingers from a distance.

It had been this way for the last hour.

After spending the end of the afternoon with Steph, he'd taken off for more recon. She'd needed a break from the case, but he couldn't afford to take one, so he drove back to International Diamonds. That time Monica was at the shop, in her lab coat, studying jewels. He'd kept an eye on her from down the street, watching her when she left the store and answered a quick call as she walked along the block. When she hung up, she'd unlocked a white hatchback and headed straight to Sapphire.

He bet the phone call must have come from Ferdinand, the guy with the snake tattoo. A summons to appear before her partner. Surely, she'd be making her way to his upstairs office to plot their next steps in the diamond hunt. From Jake's post at the bar, he watched her, ready to pounce and follow her trail when she moved.

Without looking away, he set his water glass down on the counter. *Buzz.*

His back pocket vibrated, and he swiped his phone from it. Kylie's name flashed across the screen. *Shit.* He wanted to talk to her, but as he glanced quickly around the club, he realized there was no way to have this call now. He hit "Ignore," then tapped out a fast reply, letting her know he'd call her shortly.

Monica was on the move, and he was not going to lose her this time. He needed to know what she was up to, and he was determined to get a bead on her. Threading his way through the sweaty, dancing, nearly drunk crowd, he scanned the balcony as she strolled near one of the framed works of art. Her back was to him as she chatted with a tall, gray-haired man.

Tristan and Monica.

But why would he be here? Seconds later, Ferdinand appeared, joining the two of them. Jake's head swam with possibilities. But one thing remained starkly clear. He'd have to move quickly to find the diamonds, because the competition was closing in on him.

Rapidly.

Steph brushed a ruby-red daub of nail polish over her toenail. With her neck crooked to hold the phone in place, she chatted with her mother from her perch on the end of the hotel bed.

"How is everything going with Lance?" she asked in a flirty tone. "I know you were working on your downward-facing dog with him."

"Should I take your tone to mean you don't think I could be involved with someone your age?"

Steph chuckled as she spread the bristles across her big toe. The jewel-toned red was perfect, and she'd always enjoyed having freshly polished toenails before a dive tour. One of her few luxuries. "Not at all. Lance is a cute guy. It wouldn't be such a bad thing, now would it?"

Her mother laughed lightly. "If you must know, we were in fact doing yoga together because he wanted me to meet his mother. She's the landlord who handles the rent for that yoga studio. She also has space to lease inside a boutique in South Beach where she thinks I might be able to sell my necklaces."

Steph sat up straight, sliding the brush into the nail polish container. Excitement fluttered through her. "That's great, Mom. You could have your own place to sell your jewelry. Like a permanent location, so you don't have to rely on the craft fairs, right?"

"That's the goal. It's not cheap, but I think I should be able to pull together the money for this."

"That's so exciting. I can't wait for you to have your own shop. That's what you always wanted."

"I know," her mother said, a note of breathless joy in her tone. The sound thrilled Steph. After the uneven divorce settlement, something like this could really make a difference. Or maybe Eli could make the difference with his newfound generosity. "I saw Eli again today. He said something that made it seem as if he might finally start paying alimony," Steph offered.

"Did he now?" Her mother sounded skeptical. "He called me earlier, but I wasn't available to talk. I suppose I should call him back. Not that I want his money, but if he's going to offer it, I wouldn't say no."

"I hope that's what it's about. Let me know, OK?"

"Of course."

"Also, he said something about Andrew having a thing for you, Mom," Steph said as she fanned her toes with her other hand to dry the nails. "Is that for real?"

Her mother scoffed. "Eli had a streak of jealousy a mile wide. He was always convinced that Andrew had some sort of crush on me. He couldn't accept that the man merely viewed me as a friend and vice versa. We have always and only just been friends. But does that bother you?" her mother asked gently.

Steph considered the question for a brief second, then decided that whether Andrew thought her mother both pretty *and* a friend wasn't important. The fact that her stepdad was trying to be a better man was the only thing that mattered. "Nah. Doesn't bother me at all. It was just one of those random comments," she said, deciding to let it go.

"Now, tell me all about the man you mentioned the last time we spoke," her mom said. "Are you still trysting with him? How is it going?"

Steph sighed happily.

She was about to answer with any combination of "better than expected," "absolutely wonderful," "I'm falling for him big time," and then the other one. The one where she revealed her hopes that the two of them could become a real couple when this trip ended. But before she could dive into any of the options for her romantic life, the hotel phone rang.

"I need to answer that. I'll chat with you later."

After they hung up, Steph grabbed the receiver. The person at the front desk said, "I have a delivery at the front desk for Ms. Steph Anderson."

Nerves skittered through her. Who on earth knew that she was here in this hotel? "What is it?"

"I haven't opened it. But it looks like a very small box."

Did that small box contain a diamond? Was the thief having a change of heart and returning her rock? "I'll be right there."

When she arrived at the front desk a few minutes later, butterflies swarmed her chest. The last time someone had stopped by her hotel, she'd lost $10,000. A woman wearing a white-and-cranberry floral shirt and a brass hotel name tag manned the desk.

"How may I help you?" she asked.

"I'm staying in room 412. You just called about a delivery for me."

"Ah, right." The woman reached under the counter at the desk. When she popped back up, she handed Steph a small white box.

Steph narrowed her eyes. "Who left this for me?"

The woman at the desk peered at her notes. When she raised her face, she said, "Mr. and Mrs. Smith."

Steph's arm shot out, clutching the counter, holding on. The front desk swayed and bobbed, like a boat tossed in high seas. Somehow, she steadied herself and opened the box.

Inside, she found a plastic ring with a candy gem on it.

With nervous fingers, she picked up the note.

Here is your cut of the diamonds.

CHAPTER NINETEEN

She was done.

Over.

Towel thrown in.

"They won," she said when Jake returned that evening from his stakeout. After she told him about the ring, he grilled the front desk for information. The clerk simply held up her hands and said she was so sorry and she knew nothing more.

"The hotels on this island need to do a better job at policing the deliveries," he muttered as they walked away.

"I know," she said as she stuffed the candy ring in a trash can in the lobby. "I really don't want to come to the Caymans again. To think, I worked so hard to find my way back here, and now this is the last place I want to be."

"Don't say that," he said softly, brushing the back of his fingers across her cheek when they stepped into the elevator. "You love it here. Besides, this is the only place I want to be right now."

❧

She thanked him for the twentieth time.

He'd been so damn understanding of her decision. She wasn't sure why she'd been so nervous to tell him she was officially done with the diamond mission, but maybe it was because she was worried that ending this partnership would mean an end to them.

It hadn't. They were spending her last day together, enjoying the next morning in the gentle ocean waves.

Tomorrow, she left for her tour, and he'd stay behind to keep working the case. Waving the white flag hadn't been an easy choice, but it seemed the safest route at this point. Eli had promised to do right by her mom, and that was all she had truly wanted in the first place—the chance to fix the fracture in her family as best she could. Besides, she wasn't leaving all those people who'd lost money high and dry—Jake was still on the hunt for the missing funds, and frankly, he was better at it than she was.

Leave it to the pros. It simply wasn't her place anymore.

"You don't have to keep thanking me. I completely get it."

"But I really appreciate your understanding," she said as they walked out of the water and flopped down on their blanket on the white, sugary sand.

He rested a hand on her hip. That little touch sent shivers through her. "I'm not an asshole. Of course I understand. This was something you wanted to try, and it's been, for lack of a better word, a complete bust."

She laughed. "Yeah, *bust* describes it perfectly."

"And this. Describes this, too," he said, quickly darting a hand to cup one of her breasts before pulling away. "I should behave in public."

The beach was starting to fill up with couples and families, too, parking towels, buckets, and shovels on the beach. "I don't see why you'd start now," she teased.

"You're right. Screw behaving." He flicked his finger against her starfish belly ring. Her breath caught from that slight touch. He moved his fingers up her flesh, then brushed the pad of his thumb over the treasure chest necklace. "You know what would look good in this necklace?"

"What?"

"A topaz," he declared, then shook his head. "Wait. No. A peridot."

"My, my. Don't you know your gemstones."

"Again, I have two sisters."

"And they were into birthstones?"

"Of course. Kylie is August and Kate November. What are you?"

"July," she said with a lift of her eyebrow.

"I know what July is."

"And I like that it's not a diamond at all."

"How happy are you to be done with diamonds?"

"I'm happy to be done with diamonds, but not with you," she said, figuring now was as good a time as any to voice this truth. It had been on her mind since last night, since she'd spoken to her mom, since he'd said such sweet and sexy words to her in the elevator, since they'd been wrapped up in each other's arms. "I'm going to miss you, Jake Harlowe."

"Yeah, about that."

⟳

There once was a time, not so long ago, when Jake had zero interest in anything that got in the way of work. His single-minded focus to get in, do the job, and get out had been his sole motivation most days. The experience with Rosalinda had soured him on mixing romance with work, while the stockpile of tuition bills had reminded him every day that he had no room for anything but that top priority.

Then Steph Anderson walked into his life. Or more precisely, she walked into the game of darts he'd been playing solo at the Pink Pelican.

Ask him seven days ago if he'd have imagined he could fall this quickly and he'd have scoffed.

But everything about this job had surprised him. Most of all, how hard he fell for her, even as he'd tried to fight it. "We haven't talked about the elephant in the room," he said, brushing his fingers across her soft thigh. Kate had been right. He'd fallen for a woman in a bikini. But it wasn't the bikini that had made him fall so damn hard. It was the woman.

He was no longer working with her, so he was free to proceed. Hell, he'd be game to move forward with her even if they were still on the hunt together. He just wanted her, and he didn't want to fight that desire any longer.

Steph scanned the beach, pretending to search for elephants. "I don't see a pachyderm."

"No. The elephant is Florida."

"Ah, I see. And what exactly about Florida is elephantine?"

He laughed, loving her sense of humor and the way they bantered. "This. Us. The fact you and I just fit."

A smile spread across her face as she shifted closer to him. "How do we fit?"

He pulled her snug next to him. "I like to think we fit in Florida."

The look in her eyes said, *Go on.*

He counted off on his fingers. "One, we live close to each other. Two, it would be a damn shame if this," he said, gesturing from her to him, "had to end when this trip ends. Three, what would you think about seeing each other when we're back home?"

Her grin said it all. She roped her arms around his neck. "I only have one reply: yes."

He sealed their promise with a kiss under the rising morning sun, as gentle waves lapped the shore. This brief affair had started in a tropical paradise. But it wouldn't end there. This was only the beginning, and no matter what happened next with the diamonds, Jake had already won.

He had the girl. She was the real prize.

CHAPTER TWENTY

The floor mats in Eli's Audi were covered in sand from their morning beach excursion.

"I can't return the car to him like this," Steph said as she slid into the driver's seat and turned the key in the ignition.

"There's a car wash down the road," Jake said, gesturing to the right as they exited the hotel.

"Cool. I'll stop there first." She followed his directions, glancing into the rearview mirror as she slowed at a light. A streak of green metal raced past her, and she snapped her gaze to the window. "Was that a green Honda?"

But the car was already gone, zipping down a side street and out of sight. "Let's hope not," he said, scanning for the auto in question. "I don't see anything. It was probably a different car. Tell me more about your tour tomorrow. How many people?"

"I'm fully booked," she said with a grin as she pressed her foot to the gas, choosing to put the green car out of her mind. "My stepdad's assistant manager even joined the tour. Clarissa. She's super sweet. She adores Eli."

"That's nice," he said, though his tone sounded grudging.

"Sorry, I know you don't like him."

He held up his hands. "We will agree to disagree on this. I respect your need to step back, as long as you respect mine to keep going."

"Of course. And don't worry, I will keep all your secrets. I've got your back," she said.

Soon, they arrived at the car wash.

"The full deluxe, please," she said, handing the keys to an eager car-wash attendant, who wore khaki shorts, white bouncy sneakers, and a sky-blue T-shirt with the name of the car wash emblazoned across the chest.

Island Shine.

"That'll take about twenty minutes. If you'd like to wait outside, we have comfy chairs under the awning, or you can check out our lovely selection of sundries and island gifts inside," he said in a helpful tone, gesturing to a gift shop attached to the car wash. "You can even watch the cars being washed. We have a long window on one side that gives a view into the wash itself."

"Ooh," Steph said. "Can't go wrong with that."

"I do believe we'll avail ourselves of the gift shop opportunities," Jake said, dropping a hand to her back as he held open the glass door in a deliberately gallant gesture. Then to her he said, "This is our first official date, so you just better get used to this kind of fancy treatment."

She arched an eyebrow. "First date? What about the panini shop?"

He leaned in to whisper. "First date now that you've finally come to terms with the elephantine desire you possess to have more of me."

She rolled her eyes. "You are such a cocky bastard."

He answered by pinching her butt as they walked to the display that boasted a selection of up to 170 different and deliciously scented car air fresheners.

"How is this a date exactly?" she asked. "Are you going to treat me to whatever kind of air freshener my little heart desires?"

He nodded. "I'm just that kind of generous guy," he said, sweeping his arm out broadly. A huge array of scented cardboard shapes dangled along the hooks on the shelves. "Tell me. I'm dying to know more about you. What is your favorite car scent?" He reached for an air freshener shaped like a coconut. "Could it be the enticing aroma of the world's most impossible fruit to eat if stuck on a deserted island?" He grabbed a pineapple cardboard cutout. "Wait. These suckers are hard to open, too. But they are the most delicious fruit known to mankind. Please tell me you love pineapple."

"Like a house on fire."

He sighed happily and cupped his hand to her cheek. "You have impeccable taste. You like pineapple and you like me."

She laughed, enjoying the easy way he had with her, and how he could take something as mundane as waiting for a car wash and turn it into a good time.

Jake's hand shot out and he grabbed more air fresheners, brandishing them all like a fan as the car-wash machines whirred faintly, the hum of motors turning landing on her ears.

"Cherry? Cinnamon? Lavender? Wait. What about this?" He reached for one more. "Pumpkin?" He crinkled his nose and lowered his voice to a bare whisper. He spoke as a plea. "Please don't say pumpkin; please don't say pumpkin; please don't say pumpkin."

"Aha! You're one of those people who hates pumpkin spice lattes. I've heard about your kind but have never spotted one in the wild."

He nodded vigorously. "So much. I can't stand pumpkin spice lattes or pumpkin bread or pumpkin pie. It feels so good to confess this to you. And you need to know this to be with me, but I don't understand the pumpkin craze. Please say you understand," he said, grasping her hand.

She adopted a reassuring tone. "No need to worry. I will never force a pumpkin on you."

He wiped his hand across his forehead. "OK, back to the air fresheners. Take your pick. You can even get two if you want. I'm splurging."

She drummed her fingers against her chin. "I'm going for cherry and also coconut. In part because I know coconut drives you wild," she said, bringing her fingertips to the front of his shirt and tap-dancing a line down his chest.

⁓

He grabbed her hand, laced his fingers through hers. "How did you know?"

"Because my lotion is coconut sugar, and you're always sniffing me and groaning in pleasure."

Nailed it.

He yanked her close and ran his nose from her collarbone up the column of her neck, inhaling her intoxicating smell. He was aroused instantly. "You're right," he whispered and flicked his tongue lightly against the shell of her ear. She melted into his touch, and the way she fused her body to his, even here, even in a car-wash gift shop, reinforced that trying a relationship on for size simply felt . . . right.

So damn right.

Ironic, too, because a week ago he was dead sure he'd be able to keep this fling no-strings. He'd been certain he wouldn't break his rule about getting involved with someone he worked with. But the thought of being without Steph was more terrifying than snakes. He wanted all in, all strings attached.

She was some kind of special, and now, she was some kind of his.

He wanted to know even more about her. He wanted to know every detail, so he could do sweet little things for her when he saw her back home. Bring her gifts. Take her out. Make her feel adored. He rounded the corner to the greeting card row.

"My Steph education must continue. Greeting cards. Do you get the ones that are all heartfelt and gooey, or the ones that mock the person's age?"

She shook her head. "Neither. I usually go for black-and-white comics of animals saying something clever. Or ones that mock cats. Because cats are, let's be honest, kind of mockable."

"Totally mockable. Because cats can be assholes."

"There should be a greeting card for that: Sorry I behaved like a cat."

He laughed, then dropped a quick kiss on her forehead. "You're a perfect woman. I can barely take your awesomeness."

He rounded the endcap, passing a display of Island Shine T-shirts on their way into the next aisle. This row carried car accoutrements, from steering wheel covers to windshield wipers to maps. "Map or GPS?"

"GPS, of course. But if I were ever traveling through Europe, I would wing it and go without either, because that would be fun."

"That's it. I'm going to have to take you to Europe so we can travel without a map or GPS."

"I won't say no to that."

He grabbed her hand and marched to the final aisle, with candy on one side, cold treats on the other. "Ghirardelli or Godiva?"

"Ghirardelli. Hold the nuts," she said with a wink. "What about you? You'd probably say both. Given your overactive sweet tooth."

He fixed her with a stare. "My sweet tooth is a very serious condition. I would appreciate you not making fun of it. Once when I was a young boy and lost a tooth, the tooth fairy took my sweet tooth by mistake. It was the most devastating week of my life. She had to return it, and when she did, all hope was restored to the world."

"You are a piece of work, Jake Harlowe."

He looped a hand around her waist, unable to resist touching her. "So are you," he said, nuzzling her neck. "Have I mentioned how glad I am that this isn't over?"

She nodded into him. "Yes."

"So glad," he said softly, then looked her in the eyes. "It won't always be easy to see each other. I travel a lot, and I know you do, too, for work, but I want to do everything I can to make this work."

"Me, too," she whispered.

He wrapped her tighter in an embrace and brushed soft kisses across her cheek. He hardly cared where they were. He'd kiss her anywhere. He wanted her fiercely.

As his lips brushed her skin, a flash of movement caught his eye. Craning his neck, he peered at the rectangular window that looked into the car wash itself.

The black flaps brushed aimlessly back and forth, slowing their pace against a car. The whirring of the machine faded, then clicked off. As the motion ceased, a pair of car-wash attendants stepped gingerly through the machinery, inspecting the car.

The gleaming black Audi.

"Your stepdad's car," he said, pointing. "Something's wrong with it."

She stared through the window, then spun around. "I should go see."

He left the air freshener at the counter. "Be right back for this."

He shielded his eyes as they walked outside, then to the entrance of the car-wash machine. One of the attendants had slid a long iron hook underneath Eli's car, as if he were trying to attach it to the chassis.

"Looks like it's stuck," Steph said to him.

A grunt sounded from the attendant as he yanked, muscles straining against the back of his shirt.

"A little more," the other guy called out. He was the one who'd greeted them.

"Hey there," Jake said loudly. "That's our car. Everything OK?"

The attendant looked up, nodded, and flashed a smile. "Yes. Please don't worry. The car just got stuck on the rails while it was going through. Happens once in a while, but we're getting it out."

"Why did it get stuck?" Steph asked curiously.

"Ah, sometimes it happens when the trunk is heavy. This one seems to be lower to the ground than usual," the attendant said, then returned to helping his coworker tug the Audi free from the machines.

But Jake wasn't thinking about the machines anymore. He was thinking only about *why* a vehicle would ride so low. There was one reason, and one reason only. Something was in it. A kernel of hope resurfaced in him, rolling through his veins, picking up speed.

He tugged at the waistband of Steph's tank top, gently pulling her out of earshot under the awning. Lowering his voice, he whispered, "Are you thinking what I'm thinking?"

Her eyes twinkled, but a hint of nerves shone through. "I'm not sure. What are you thinking?"

"I'm thinking about what might be so heavy in the trunk that it makes a car ride that low . . ." He raised his eyebrows, waiting for her to say it. Wondering if this changed her mind. Hoping it did.

Hell, he wanted to crack this case wide open with her by his side.

"Let's look inside."

CHAPTER
TWENTY-ONE

As he pulled back the heavy trunk cover, she gasped quietly, covering her mouth.

Holy shit.

He was right.

With the car now parked at the back of the car-wash lot, and the attendants vacuuming the mats, Steph was free to peek. And what an eyeful it was. Her stepfather had built a safe into the trunk of his car. Her mind scrambled with possibilities. Her brain lit up with far too many options. She'd abandoned the hunt yesterday. It had become too dangerous, but it had also stirred up too much guilt for her. The lunch with Eli had left her swimming in a sea of doubt.

She was still treading water. Only now there was a safe before her eyes, a safecracker by her side, and the potent possibility that he could finally have what he was hunting.

Talk about a dilemma.

Her gut twisted. She didn't want to find diamonds. She wanted Eli to be the guy he was becoming, the man who was changing.

"I don't know what to do," she whispered, nerves threading through her voice. Her stepfather had given her use of this car because he trusted her. She was one of the few people he trusted. To paw through his private property seemed wrong now. He might have done some shady stuff in his lifetime, but she didn't have to do the same.

"It's right here," Jake pressed. "What if, Steph? What if?"

"What if it's another trick?" she pointed out in a low tone.

"We'll never know unless we check."

Her eyes floated closed for a second. Her worries gnawed at her. This just felt . . . wrong. She opened her eyes. The noise from the vacuum grew louder, but she kept her voice low. "I won't stop you, but I don't know if I can do this."

He sighed heavily. "Seriously?"

"I know Eli's made mistakes, but he's trying to change, and it seems wrong of me to look for diamonds now."

He scrubbed a hand across his jaw. "You said you weren't going to stand in the way," he muttered, sounding irritated.

"I'm not," she said insistently. "You can go ahead. Look."

"Shit," he said as the attendants moved to the backseat now, pressing hoses to the floor of the car. "I can't look now. You're making me feel bad for trying to finish this."

She pointed at herself, and her jaw fell open. "I'm making you feel bad? It's all my fault now? C'mon. Take a little responsibility for your own emotions."

He straightened his shoulders. "Oh, excuse me for having some. Excuse me for wanting something."

"Oh, don't get all worked up about it. You're a grown man. You can deal with feeling bad, and you can also deal with trying to do your job. Doesn't mean I have to."

He crossed his arms. "I can't do it. I just can't. It's your stepdad's car, and if you don't want to, I'll have to go along with you," he said, blowing out a long stream of air. "Gotta respect my girl."

Something about the way he said that rankled her. It wasn't the use of *girl*. That didn't bother her. It was the way he tossed the decision back on her. That was wholly unfair. Frustration rushed through her, driven by the need to put a fork in this once and for all. "Look, if you won't man up, I'll do it. I'm sure it's an obvious combo like his birthday," she said, bending her head into the trunk and pressing numbers into the dial pad. But the door wiggled before she entered the last number. It wasn't even locked.

She grabbed the handle and yanked it open as the sound of the vacuum shut off.

Holy mother of jewels.

Diamonds. Everywhere. Handfuls of them. Gobs of them. Her throat went dry, and her pulse spiked. There they were. A towering pile of priceless gems, glittering in the sun. She froze, gawking at the glory before her.

She dared tilt her head an inch to catch Jake's gaze, and he was staring into the trunk in amazement, too.

"Gorgeous," he whispered in a stunned voice.

"It wasn't even locked," she said, surprised, as a door nearby slammed shut. Steph raised her face out of the trunk, looking for the source of the sound.

The click of an engine turning over blasted through the air, and the Audi took on a life of its own.

"Thanks for the help. You're the best," a woman wearing an Island Shine T-shirt shouted, and Steph raced around the car. Clarissa poked her head out the window and grinned madly at Steph. With one hand on the wheel, she peeled out of the parking lot and drove off with the car, the stash, and the keys that had been left in the ignition as the attendants cleaned.

Jake tore off after her, running like a track star, sprinting on a mad dash for the car. He ran like a bullet, powered by adrenaline. Out of the lot, down the street, chasing the black automobile.

But Clarissa and the Audi were far faster. She sped through the light by the car wash, leaving Jake in the dust. He parked his hands on his thighs and bent over, panting.

A green Honda drove by next, following the Audi. Tristan was at the wheel.

⁂

He ate his scream of frustration. Clenching his fists, he brought them to his eyes and just cursed everything and everyone under the sun. He was ready to stomp his feet, to bang his head against a door, to yank out his hair.

Because . . . fuck.

The diamonds had been in his grasp. Inches away. He'd been reaching for them when Clarissa had torn off in Steph's father's car.

It was Venice all over again. He had his hands on the goddamn prize and it was stolen from under his nose.

By Clarissa. Who was joining Steph's tour. Who Steph said was super sweet. Followed by Tristan. Steph had dined at his restaurant twice.

His chest burned. His jaw clenched. Déjà vu descended on him and gripped him hard.

Fool me once, shame on you. Fool me twice, shame on me.

He knew better, and he'd gone in anyway. He'd taken the risk for the woman, letting his stupid heart lead, and look where it had landed him.

Straight into *His Dumbass Romantic Decisions—the Sequel.*

"Did you know?" he asked, and he wasn't even sure where the words came from or what he was trying to say.

"What?" She looked at him like he was crazy.

He pointed in Clarissa's direction, though she was long gone, and so was her accomplice. "Did you know she was going to do that?"

She parked her hands on her hips. "How would I know that?"

"How else would she know to be here?"

"She was following us," Steph said, as if it were obvious.

But was it? Was it crystal clear? Or was it muddy? "You said she was joining your dive tour. You said she was nice. You said you liked her."

"And that means what, Jake?" she asked, her tone cool and even.

"How can you be so casual about her taking the diamonds? Unless you're—"

She held up a hand. "Think real hard before you say it. Ask yourself if you want to go there."

"Go where?" he volleyed back.

"You're about to suggest I'm in on it, aren't you?"

"I don't know what the fuck to think," he spat out, frustration eating away at every bit of common sense, spitting out every cell in his brain. He mimed holding something precious. "I had them. We had them. And then she just took off. In your stepfather's car. I've been there before, Steph, and you knew it. I told you what happened in Venice."

"And somehow that means I'm in on it? What the hell? You think I plotted that with my stepdad's assistant manager, who I just met a few days ago?"

"Did you, though? Did you just meet her? Or have you known her for years like you know everyone else on this island?" he said, because he didn't know what the hell to think anymore. For all he knew, he'd been played a fool from the start. What if she'd backed out last night for this very reason? To set up this moment? To make herself appear more unlikely as a thief? That's what Rosalinda had done.

He'd thought he knew Steph, but what the hell did he know about anything? This was his Achilles' heel—he fell too hard and too fast for the wrong women.

Women who crossed him.

"I don't know her. She's *clearly* the thief. She's *clearly* been after the diamonds all along. She *clearly* followed us," Steph said, her chin raised high. She stabbed her finger against the side of her skull. "How is this not *clear* to you? How is this not getting through your head? I did not plan a diamond heist with Clarissa. She was just going to join me on a dive."

"Maybe a celebratory tour?"

"Are you crazy?"

He couldn't think straight. He couldn't see straight. Nothing made sense anymore. He'd run into dead ends every damn step of the way. He'd been thwarted everywhere and none of the clues had added up. She could have been using him as her front man to break into places and chase down leads 'til she got closer. Hell, she might be working with Monica, too. Maybe Monica had staked him out for Steph.

He didn't know.

But he knew this—there was no proof her own diamond had been stolen. Only her word.

"Where's your diamond, Steph?" he asked, his tone low and accusing. She'd pointed fingers first. She was certain he'd pilfered her rock. But maybe it had never been stolen. "How do I even know for sure it was stolen? How do I know you haven't been playing me from the get-go?"

Her eyes widened. "I thought we'd gone over this already, but just in case it's not clear. I like you, Jake. I'm crazy for you. I did not play you."

"But how do I know for sure? How do I know if any of this between us is real? Or just a setup to take the diamonds?"

She opened her mouth to speak, but no words came. Just a low hiss of breath.

Then, words came. Measured. Focused. Sharp as a blade. "One, you know because of the time we've spent together. Two, it's not a setup because I'm falling for you. Three, in case the first two weren't clear"—she paused and waved crisply at him—"that hurts more than you can know. Good-bye."

CHAPTER
TWENTY-TWO

His. Hers. Stolen. Owned. Doctored. Legit evidence. $10 million or $10,000.

None of those specifics mattered right now. Steph had spent enough time trying to figure out what was up with the diamonds and who'd taken what from whom.

But right now, she wasn't an amateur private detective, a treasure hunter, or a Robin Hood. She was a daughter who'd taken her father's car and lost something precious.

That was the only truth, and that's how she had to behave as her cab pulled up to Eli's house thirty minutes later.

He hadn't even freaked out when she'd called and told him why she was taking a cab. That his car and millions in diamonds were stolen by Clarissa. He'd simply said, "Not to worry, my dear. I'll take care of it."

She dug into her purse to pay the driver, hunting for bills in her wallet. When she raised her face, Eli was at the window, handing the driver a fifty.

She unbuckled, opened the door, and got out of the car. He gave her a peck on the cheek. "You are a sight for sore eyes," he declared, and his grin seemed to stretch to the moon.

"Your car was stolen. Your diamonds are gone. Why are you in such a happy mood?" she asked, knitting her brow together.

He placed a hand on her back and gestured to the stone path. "Come inside. Let's have some champagne with Isla. We have lots to celebrate."

Once inside, Isla practically pummeled Steph with a hug. "You're a superstar."

Perhaps she'd waltzed into a fun house. Down was up, right was left, and her stepfather was celebrating having been robbed. Steph furrowed her brow. "How am I a superstar? Somebody needs to explain what's going on."

"First, champagne," Isla said, her voice as bubbly as the beverage that she poured from a bottle of Dom Pérignon.

Eli handed her the flute. "A toast. To you."

Steph raised her glass, succumbing to the topsy-turvy world she'd entered. Clearly, Eli would tell her when he was good and ready.

"Isla and I promised that we'd only open this bottle when we cracked the case," he said, lifting a glass to his lips and taking a sip.

"What do you mean? The case?"

Isla's eyes lit up. "The case of who's been trying to steal the diamonds."

"Oh. So you knew that . . . ," Steph started, letting her voice trail off. No need to admit she'd been hunting those jewels, too. Her motive was different, after all. She'd been trying to help him, in a roundabout way—to save him from others.

"A few weeks ago, it became clear that someone was sniffing around for our precious gems," Eli said, leaning against the marble kitchen counter, draping an arm around his fiancée. She lifted her hand and laced her fingers through his.

"This started a few weeks ago?" she repeated. That was well before she and Jake had arrived on the island.

He nodded. "We've done everything we can to try to catch a thief. And now we have. Seconds after you called, I contacted my friends on the police force about the stolen car and the stolen gems, and Clarissa is already under arrest."

Isla squeezed his arm. "Don't forget Tristan is, too," she said.

"He was such a dunce," Eli said with a laugh. "That chocolate drink was awful, wasn't it? He knows how to make great food, but he can't seem to stop there. Keeps trying to become some bizarre mixologist as well."

Steph made a timeout sign. "Back it up. You're telling me that Clarissa and Tristan were working together to steal your diamonds?"

"Seems they were. I had a hunch it was her," Eli said, stopping to drink some of the champagne. "I've been trying to catch her. That's why Ferdinand put nuts in the back of the frame in my office, and then dropped hints all over the club that the diamonds were in my frame. Clarissa must have been so shocked when she sliced open the frame the other day and found nothing but nuts," Eli said, cracking up, clutching his belly.

Isla joined in. "Oh my God, I would pay good money to have seen the look on her face."

Steph's cheeks flamed bright red, and she stared at her feet, hoping, praying they wouldn't notice that she'd become a beet. But they seemed to believe Clarissa had been the one to take the nuts from the frame, not her. That presumption made sense. Clarissa was indeed the thief, and Steph was right, too, that her stepdad had been one step ahead, planting fake clues all along. But why? Some details didn't add up.

"What about Ferdinand?" Steph asked. "The guy with the snake tattoo? I thought you were concerned he might have taken your necklace, Isla?"

Isla shook her head. "He's lovely."

"Ferdie is my right-hand man," Eli chimed in. "I pay him well, and he uses it to support his family. He wouldn't bite the hand that feeds him. He's been helping me all along to lay the groundwork."

"But Marie said something to me the other night," Steph began, then stopped talking because she didn't want to get Marie in trouble.

"Oh, Marie is involved with him. They're dating," Eli said. "So she helped to plant the possibility that it was him. We figured if the real thief thought it was Good Ol' Ferdie, he or she might be more cavalier, and she was."

The sunlight streamed through the kitchen window and splashed its rays across Isla. A glint of blue flashed on her throat. "Your necklace. It's back. Was that returned?"

Isla placed her hand on it, then stage-whispered. "It was never missing in the first place. I just pretended it was stolen by wearing a fake."

"But you said everyone at your gallery party was looking for it?" Steph asked, still trying to process the scope of their cleverness.

Isla rubbed her thumb and forefinger across the gem. "I loosened it in the casing before the party. When I freshened up my drink, I leaned over the glass, the gem fell in, and voilà. Everyone went looking for it, but Eli swooped in to take my drink and keep my engagement diamond safe and sound."

"So you weren't really calling insurance? Were you lying to me about that?" Steph asked, turning to Eli. She knew she didn't have the right to feel tricked, given what she'd been trying to pull off.

Still, she sure as hell felt hoodwinked. And that feeling stung like a yellow jacket, since she'd been looking out for Eli. Even when she'd been cloak-and-daggering it, she'd done it all to try to exonerate him, to try to save him from more trouble.

"Clarissa insisted upon it. As soon as she heard about the 'missing diamond,' she made a big stink about how I had to call insurance. Probably to make herself seem less likely as the culprit. So I called and reported it missing."

"And you're going to call now and tell them you found it?"

He shrugged happily. "Sure, I suppose I ought to do that."

Something raged inside her over his cavalier attitude. On the one hand, she understood why he was so gleeful. Someone had been trying to take something precious to him, and he'd laid a clever trap. But was that something even his to begin with?

All of a sudden, Isla pointed frantically to the counter. She covered her mouth with her hand and whispered in terror, "Spider."

Eli leaped into action, grabbing a paper towel and squashing it instantly. He brandished the wadded-up towel with the dead bug. "Victory again."

"Oh thank God," Isla said, breathing out in relief. "I hate spider season."

Steph couldn't care less about spiders, so she returned to the matter at hand. "So who stole my diamond?"

Eli cocked his head to the side. "Your diamond was taken?"

"Yes. No faking there. It was taken from my hotel room," she said, and explained how they'd pulled it off.

Eli banged a fist against his counter. "Bastard! Tristan must have seen me give it to you at the restaurant that day. That's how he knew you had one. Dammit. I wish that hadn't happened to you."

"Yeah, me, too."

"And all because of a sour business deal. And for Clarissa, she wanted the money to pay off college debt. If she'd have just asked me, I'd have given her the money."

A sense of déjà vu washed over Steph. While she had no affection for Clarissa, the statement felt oddly familiar. He'd said something similar to her at their first lunch—if she'd only told him about her business trouble, he'd have helped her out. But it was easy to make that sort of offer after the fact.

"Would you have, though?"

"Given it to her? Of course."

"Just like you're going to start paying Shelly the alimony?"

"Um," he said, gazing at the ceiling and scratching his head. "Did I say I was going to give her alimony?"

"Yes," Steph said emphatically, waving her arms. "Yes. You said you weren't fair to her. You said you wanted to be more equitable. You told me that," she said, her voice rising as she sensed him erecting his Teflon wall once more.

"Eli," Isla said softly, wrapping a hand around his arm. "Remember what we talked about?"

"Yeah. About being more generous," Steph said, chiming in.

"That wasn't exactly it."

"What was it, then?"

"We just don't think it's wise to discuss money matters. My family never did, and it's best if we just keep some matters private," she said.

Steph studied Isla's face. Her pretty eyes. Her gorgeous cheeks. In some weird way, she'd liked the woman. Isla had been sweet and kind. But today, the whole *it's-private* act bugged her.

"Private? Like the money you took from your company is private?" she said, directing it to both of them.

Isla's eyes widened, and she cast her gaze downward instantly. "Eli," she whispered, then dropped her voice even more and mouthed silently to her fiancé, *You told her?*

Steph's world stopped spinning. Her features froze. There it was. The admission. The confession. The very possibility she'd fought like hell to deny and protested kicking and screaming. Hunting, sneaking around, leaving no stone unturned, she'd hoped against hope that the father she knew was the real Eli, and that it had all been a mistake. She'd devoted a whole goddamn week of her time, and countless pieces of her heart, to searching for a truth that was a lie.

He wasn't innocent after all.

He'd fucking done it, and he'd gotten away with it. Her insides felt hollow, carved out by the blade of his lies.

He squeezed Isla's fingers. "Shush, it's OK." Then to Steph, "We need to move on from these money matters."

"How c-could—?" she began, sputtering. She wanted to dig into it with him. To ask him how the hell he could take money from innocent people. How he could steal the retirement funds he was entrusted with. But she knew if she uttered those words, he'd shut her down even further. She sucked them inside, swallowed them, and asked another question.

"Where are the diamonds? Did you get them back from your car?"

Eli laughed and waved a hand dismissively. "No need to worry about those. The real ones are safe and sound and so well hidden that no one will figure it out. Didn't even need to put them in a bank."

Her head clanged. She grabbed the counter to hold on. "Wait. So those diamonds in your trunk were fake?"

He nodded.

Steph's mind rewound to an hour before. To the gorgeous gleam of the jewels in a safe in the car. They had looked as real as anything. But then again, a car *was* an odd place to store diamonds. "If the diamonds in the back of your car were fake, where are the real ones?"

He nodded proudly. "Real ones are still safe and sound. I put the fakes ones there in the hopes that Clarissa would go after the car. I would never put real ones in my car. That's why I gave it to you."

She gripped the counter harder. "Not because it was hot? Not because of the air-conditioning?"

"Well, that did play a role, too. Did you enjoy the air-conditioning?"

She parted her lips to speak, but she was a fish, sucking air. She wasn't sure how to even respond to such an incredulous question. She went with a simple truth. "Yes. It was nice and cool. But I think it's kind of crummy that you used me as bait."

"Now, dear, I had a feeling she was following you, and I wanted to catch her quickly and we did. I've been dropping hints that the diamonds were in the car. This was the fastest way to solve the crime. You're my little crime fighter."

She blinked as she tried to wrap her head around this latest piece of information. "You thought she'd go after them so you gave me your car?" She stabbed a finger against her chest for emphasis. "You didn't care about my safety?"

Isla cut in, trying to reassure. "Darling, we knew Clarissa wouldn't hurt you. She's a nice girl who just needed money for bills."

"That's beside the point. You had no idea what she would do. Or Tristan for that matter."

"But you're here; you're just fine. And I would never do anything to harm you," Eli said as he raised his champagne flute in a toast. "Let's celebrate. The diamonds are safe, the thieves have been caught, and you helped us. What more could we possibly want? The one nagging little issue is that she stole your diamond. But I can give you another one."

"I don't want another diamond. I don't want a diamond at all. That's the last thing I want."

"Then take my watch," he said, holding out his wrist and offering his Rolex.

"I don't want a watch, either."

Steph's head felt like it was made of cotton. Her legs were jelly. She needed to get out of here, far away from him.

She stumbled out the door, shocked that she'd been so wrong about him. She'd believed desperately in a second chance, and that completely misplaced faith in her stepfather had driven a pickax between her and the man she'd fallen for.

But Jake had delivered the punishing blow with his utter lack of faith in her.

CHAPTER
TWENTY-THREE

He walked.

He walked the entire length of Seven Mile Beach. Fine, that wasn't some huge feat of physical fitness, but he needed to burn off his frustration. He was mad about the case. Mad about the way everything had come up empty.

Most of all, he was angry with himself.

As he neared the end of the beach, he grabbed his phone from his pocket and called Kylie. That was the one relationship he couldn't fuck up. She'd texted him earlier that she had good news.

"Hey, how was the test? How's the tutor?"

"It's all going well. I got an A on my test. Can you believe it?"

He beamed. "Yes, I can believe it, and that's awesome. I'm so proud of you. I knew you could do it."

"It was all thanks to your friend. That woman who helped me the other night."

He stopped in his tracks, the ocean crashing against the shore. "It was?"

Kylie's enthusiasm could be felt through the phone line. "Yes, half the test wound up being on the topic she helped me with. I wouldn't have been able to figure it out without her help."

"Wow," he said, and resumed his pace. The reminder of Steph gnawed at him. She'd tricked him. She'd set him up. How could she be so damn sweet to his sister and still stab him in the back?

"I'm glad you did well, Kylie."

"Is she your girlfriend? I like her."

"No. She's not," he said through gritted teeth. "Well, she was for about an hour."

"Oh no. What did you do to mess it up?"

"Hey now. Why would you assume I messed it up?" he said as he ducked down a side street that looked familiar.

"Because you're you. Because you're a man. And because you don't always trust people, so sometimes you assume the worst about them."

"Ha. Thanks for pigeonholing me due to my gender," he said as he passed a café and an ice-cream shop.

"You didn't answer the question. What did you do to mess it up?"

"Nothing. We had a misunderstanding."

"Well, do you like her?"

He heaved a sigh. "I did. A lot. But then something happened."

"Did she cheat on you?"

"No," he said quickly.

"Then I'm guessing it can be fixed. And she's really awesome, and if she's the first woman in years you're calling a girlfriend, I think you need to try to fix things."

"I'll take it under advisement," he said, then stopped walking when he realized where his feet had taken him. The Pink Pelican. "Hey, congrats on the A. I'll talk to you soon."

"Love you, Jake."

"Love you, too."

It was only four in the afternoon, so the joint was quiet. A few customers sipped afternoon cocktails at tables, but he had the bar to himself.

Marie slapped down a napkin and said, "What'll it be?" When she raised her face, she grinned. "Jake the fisherman! How are you?"

"I've had better days."

"Pale ale, then?"

"That'll help," he said.

She poured a beer from the tap, then set it down and parked her hands on the counter. "Fish not biting today?"

He shook his head. "Nope. Not a one."

"Bummer. Such a shame. Because it's a lovely day from where I sit."

"Yeah? Why's that?" he asked, bringing the glass to his lips. Ah, this cool beer was the one bright spot in his shitty afternoon.

"My boyfriend got a promotion and a raise."

Jake lifted his glass in a toast to Marie's man. "Congrats. That's always nice to hear."

"I'm so proud of him. He helped to catch a thief."

The glass nearly slipped from his hands. "Sorry. What did you say?"

"Remember that robbery I told you about the other night?"

"Of course," he said quickly, eager to get to the news.

"It was all a setup to catch the real thief. Turns out that the assistant manager at Sapphire tried to steal some diamonds today from Mr. Thompson. But they were fake. Too bad for her. And she's in jail, so it really is too bad for her."

He gripped the edge of the bar, shock radiating through him. "Who's your boyfriend?"

"Ferdinand Costello," she said, and cartoon birds seemed to chirp in happiness as she said his name. "He did everything he could to help catch Clarissa and Tristan. They're both behind bars now. The police move fast in this town when it comes to helping Eli Thompson."

"I'll say," he said, then he picked up his phone. He had no clue what to say to Steph, but he needed to find a way to apologize.

Wait. That was wrong. He had to do way more than say he was sorry.

He had to get down on his knees and grovel. He'd been dead wrong at the car wash. He'd flown off the handle and accused her wildly of something she hadn't done. All because of his past, his wounds, his own prideful emotional scars. That was no way to start a new relationship.

He started to dial her when his phone rang. She was calling him. Hope dared to surface inside him. Maybe the two of them were fixable. Maybe they'd move past this misunderstanding in a jiffy.

"Hey there," he said.

"I don't have a key to your room. All my things are there, and I need them for my trip," Steph said in a crisp, businesslike tone.

"I'll meet you at the room in thirty minutes."

He didn't have the chance to grab a bouquet of flowers to say he was sorry, but words would have to do. He paid the bar tab and hoofed it to the hotel, where he found her waiting outside room 412. Looking like the woman he was crazy about, the woman who'd helped his little sister, and the woman he'd wronged.

"Hi," he said softly.

Her arms were crossed. Her eyes were hard. Oh, she was not going to go easy on him. "Hello."

Her voice was devoid of emotion.

Sliding his key through the slot, he opened the door for her. As soon as they were inside, memories flashed before his eyes, like a reel in fast-forward, of all the other times they'd entered a hotel room. Usually, within seconds, she was up against the wall, in his arms. But this time? She turned in to the restroom, wrapped one arm around all her toiletries, and shoved them into the little bag she kept them in. With alarming speed.

He needed to move quickly.

"Steph," he said, his voice as dry as tinder. He tried again, clearing his throat. "Steph."

She marched out of the bathroom and headed straight for her suitcase. Jamming the makeup kit into the bag, she didn't even glance over her shoulder as she said, "Yes?"

"I'm sorry."

She shook her head. "No need to apologize."

Within seconds, she'd grabbed the few sundresses and tank tops that weren't already in her suitcase and stuffed them inside. She zipped it up.

"I'm really sorry," he continued. "I overreacted, and I shouldn't have said those things. I know you didn't set me up."

She rose and arched an eyebrow. "Yeah, how do you know that?"

"I heard what happened. I heard it from Marie. I mean, just a few details. But she told me that Clarissa was arrested."

The corners of her lips curved into a grin, but the smile didn't reach her eyes. "Aww, that's nice that you changed your mind. I'm so glad to hear that."

"You are?" he asked, because it sure didn't sound like it.

She slung her bag on her shoulder. "Absolutely. I think it's fantastic that you *only* believed me after you heard a police report. I love that it had *nothing* to do with trusting in me. And that you only came around when you had cold, hard evidence."

He nodded once, taking his lumps like a big boy. "Fine. I get it. I'm sorry. But how is that any different than when you thought I took your diamond?" he asked, tilting his head to the side.

"You want to go there? You want to revisit that?" she asked, anger radiating off her in waves.

"Just feels like we're even and we could move on. You thought I took your diamond, and you tried to figure out if I did. I thought maybe you were trying to pull a fast one on me. Two wrongs, and all? Can we call it a truce and start over?"

She stared at him, studying his eyes. Maybe considering his offer? He crossed his fingers in hope that she'd give him another chance. That she'd see how good they could be together.

She stepped closer, raised a hand. His heart beat harder. She was going to kiss him. She cupped his cheek, ran her thumb over his jawline. Damn, he loved her touch. Just loved it. He loved so many things about her.

"I'm sorry I doubted you then. I'm truly sorry. I felt terrible for thinking that," she said softly, the anger stripped from her voice now. In its place, he heard only hope, only potential. He swore their second chance was unfurling before him. As she stroked his cheek and touched him, he was certain. "And you're right. Maybe this isn't that different. Maybe I should just let it slide and move on."

"Can we? Please?" he asked softly. Everything else on this trip was such a bust. "I just want one thing to go right here, and that one thing is you."

"And I would love to say yes to you. But there's a difference between then and now."

His heart began to sink. He swallowed, waiting for the guillotine to fall. "What is it?"

"A few nights ago, I didn't feel this way for you. But everything has changed for me, and then you questioned whether I felt anything for you. When we already told each other on the beach how we felt. That's why I just needed some time to focus on work and do what I came here to do."

He furrowed his brow. "But what changed? What's different from the time you thought I stole from you and the time I thought you were setting me up? It's all about whether we trust each other, and I'm saying let's give each other another chance."

"The difference is simple," she said softly, then she inched closer and brushed her lips to his. A soft, barely there kiss that stole the breath from his lungs. That knocked his emotions into orbit. That turned everything upside down. She let go and looked him in the eyes. "I hadn't fallen in love with you then. But now I have. That's why it hurts so much more that you thought that about me." Her voice broke as her words latched onto his heart. The wheels in his brain began to turn, to pick up speed, as he tried to figure out how to give voice to this tornado of emotions touching down in his own heart.

"And that's also why I need to go."

Before he could say a word, she left.

CHAPTER
TWENTY-FOUR

She spent the night at Devon's. He ordered a pizza, and they watched the first thirty minutes of *Talladega Nights* before she fell asleep on his couch, curled up under a blanket. Sometime in the middle of the night, she kicked it off. The sliding glass door to his deck had been left open, and a breeze drifted in. Warm and tropical. A kiss from the Caymans. She stirred and sat up on the couch, hooking her arm over the side and staring out the open doors into the night.

Like this, when the beaches were quiet and the sounds of the day were folded up into sleep, the ocean was at its most constant state. A steady drumbeat against the shore. The ceaseless *whoosh* of midnight waves crashing into the sand. The pull of the tides.

High above, the moon shone, casting spotlights over the black licorice soup of the sea.

She breathed in deeply, inhaling the salty air, letting it soothe her. She imagined tossing her sadness about Eli out in the ocean, allowing the endless waters to carry it away, like a message in a bottle that would someday wash up on a distant shore. She'd harbored a false hope for so long, but yet, she didn't regret having tried to preserve at least one good memory of him. She would, however, have regretted it more if she hadn't tried. A calmness settled into her bones, knowing she'd done all she could for the man who'd raised her. She had to be at peace with his choices and with her own.

And she was. She finally was.

But when it came to Jake, she had no answers. She wasn't sure what to make of him. She was glad, though, that she'd shared her heart with him.

As she sank back down into the pillows, pushing the blanket to her calves, she spotted the light on her phone flashing. Grabbing it, she checked quickly for messages. A few sales alerts from Etsy. A note from Lance about a sunset tour in a week. She responded quickly that she'd be back and ready. She scrolled to an e-mail from the ladies who'd been on the stingray private trip earlier in the week. The sister in the purple bikini wrote that she had friends in the Caymans who wanted to do a scuba tour in three days and was that too late? Another note from an earlier inquiry asked if she was still available for a snorkel trip to Eden Rock.

At three in the morning, she smiled and tapped out her replies, confirming yes and yes. She extended her trip and settled back into slumber, grateful that her business seemed back on track. She'd come to the Caymans with only one tour booked, and she'd landed another two, and one more at home.

A star winked in the night sky.

Maybe her luck was turning.

∽

He called Andrew. Told him the latest. He hated ditching a case, but this one was getting far too slippery even for his adventuresome taste. Cops were involved. Arrests were made. The target was onto it. He could smell the ending if he kept on pressing, and it smelled like the kind of trouble he didn't need in his life. The kind that would land him on the wrong side of the law. In his line of work, he tangoed with that possibility often enough as he bent the rules. One more bend, and he'd break.

"Hey, you gave it your best shot, and I appreciate that," Andrew said.

"Sorry, man. I really wanted to deliver for you."

"Me, too," he said with a sigh. "But that's the way the cookie crumbles. Sometimes, you can't right a wrong."

A pang of regret lodged inside Jake. "Truer words," he said.

"Besides, it's probably time for me to go to the SEC and let them know what happened. I've been trying to deal with this under the radar, but sometimes you need to call for backup."

"I hear ya, man. I'm guessing it's time."

"You heading back home?"

"I've got a flight out of town tonight."

"I'll send you the final payment," Andrew said, and Jake liked being paid but hated being paid for work he couldn't deliver. He said good-bye, shouldered his bag, and headed to the door of his hotel room.

As he put his hand on the knob, his phone rang. He grabbed it from his pocket and slid his thumb over the screen when he saw it was Kate.

"Are you all packed up and ready to fly?"

"I am indeed."

"Can you unpack and stay one more night?"

"Why? Don't tell me it's about Eli Thompson because I just got off the phone with Andrew."

"Nope," she said, a burst of enthusiasm in her tone. "New gig. Just got a call from a corporate bigwig. His nineteen-year-old son is in the Caymans partying it up too hard. He wants to get him out of there and back home before he causes more trouble. The client is in California, so he figures we can get to his son faster than he can."

"What's the catch?" Jake asked, his antennae up, as he set down his bag.

"No catch. Just find the guy. I've got a few leads as to where he's been seen. Should be easy."

He scoffed. "The last job was supposed to be easy. It wasn't."

"Oh, excuse me. Did you go into this line of work because it's simple? Get over it. Move on. Some jobs pan out, and some don't."

"Fine," he huffed. She was right. He couldn't let his frustrations over Eli affect his approach. Time to move on to the next gig. Besides, he wasn't annoyed about work. He was annoyed he'd fucked up so badly with Steph. "Give me the details."

In the morning, Devon handed her a steaming cup of coffee. "You need fuel," he said.

"I do."

She downed the coffee, crunched into some toast, then showered and dressed. "I'm ready. Thanks again for letting me stay here."

"You are welcome anytime," he said, then patted her on the back as she left to meet her group on the dock, along with the crew for the tour. She'd shoved all thoughts of Jake, diamonds, and heartbreaking stepfathers out of her head. Her sole focus centered on showing her customers how beautiful the islands were. Judging from the sheer number of underwater pictures they took, the smiles on their faces, and the thank-yous she received, she'd done her job. From the caves at Bloody Bay to the parrot fish under the sea, the ocean revived her spirits and reminded her that doing what she loved mattered most.

She'd brought her happy place to others, and for a couple of days it was their happy place, too.

Twenty-eight hours later, he'd found the party boy drunk and sleeping it off at Happy Turtle Cove. Five hours after that, he'd put the guy on a flight back to the United States. And ten minutes later, the dude's dad called to thank him.

"This means the world to me. I can't thank you enough for finding my son," the man said.

"Happy to help. Glad he's on his way back home."

"I'm at the airport already, even though he doesn't arrive for a few hours."

"Good luck," Jake said, and it was an easy job, but also a surprisingly rewarding one. Sure, the kid needed some sense knocked into him. And yeah, he needed to stop drinking. But he had a family who cared enough to try to help him. Jake hoped that made the difference in the kid's life.

He exited the airport to return to his own hotel, and this time he planned to check out for good. The two extra days had been fine, but sleeping in the same room without the woman of his dreams had, to put it mildly, sucked. He couldn't wait to return to Key Largo and crash in his own bed. Once he was home, he'd figure out a way to properly apologize to Steph. To try again. She'd clearly needed the space, but he had things he wanted to say to her, and he couldn't risk fucking it up again. A good night's rest would help reset his mind. Briefly, he wondered what had become of Monica. He hadn't seen her following him since Clarissa had been cuffed. But that made sense, he reasoned. Monica and Clarissa had been after the same prize, so Monica had no need to follow Jake anymore.

His stomach rumbled as he pulled onto the main road. Up ahead, a convenience store beckoned to him, so he parked and popped in to grab a snack. A bag of pretzels sounded reasonable enough, so he grabbed one and headed for the counter. A cardboard cutout of a coconut behind the counter caught his eye.

A grin took shape across his face as an idea popped into his head fully formed. No need to wait to see her in Florida. The present was now.

Checking the time on his phone, he realized he had an hour before Steph returned from her tour. She'd finish at Stingray City, and he'd have to grovel like he'd never groveled before. He'd acted rash, assuming the worst about Steph because of his fears. But he had to let go of the way Rosalinda had deceived him. He had to move forward, not remain stuck in the hurt of the past. Life was full of risks, and so was love. She was a risk worth taking.

So he went to the car wash.

⁀⦾

Her neck was bare. Somewhere in the ocean lay her treasure chest. She didn't know when she'd lost her necklace, but it had fallen off under the sea. Maybe someone would find a buried treasure at last.

No point in worrying about it. She'd ask her mom to make her a new one. After she said good-bye to the last of the group on the dock, she called her mother.

"Tell me everything. How did it go?"

"It was amazing," Steph said, unable to contain the smile that spread as she thought of the last thirty-six hours. She shared the highlights as she finished packing gear in her Jeep, parked in the lot near Devon's snorkel shop. She had some snorkels of his to return. "But I lost my treasure chest necklace, so I was wondering if you know an amazing jewelry craftswoman who could make me a new one?"

"Hmmm," her mother said, sounding as if she were thinking about it. "Let me see if I can come up with anyone who might possess that skill set. But you need to stop wearing that diving."

"I know. I know. I hate taking it off."

"Well, the ocean took it off for you."

"The ocean always wins." Steph pushed her sunglasses up on the bridge of her nose and slung a mesh bag on her shoulder. "Speaking of jewelry, any news on leasing that space from Lance's mom?" she asked as she closed the car door with her hip.

Her mom sighed lightly, and in that sound Steph detected a note of frustration. But her mom tried to sweep it away. "I'm working on it," she said.

"You mean you need the money for it?"

"Well, money helps," she said in a too-upbeat tone.

"What about Eli and the alimony? Did you call him back? Is he going to start paying?" she asked as she crossed the gravel lot and headed along the path to Devon's shop. The afternoon sun warmed her shoulders, and in the distance a pelican dived into the water, chasing an afternoon snack.

Her mother scoffed. "He's paying, but he's doing it in the way he thinks is best."

Steph groaned. "Oh Lord. What does that mean?"

"It means, as usual, his generosity is misdirected. The reason he called the other day was to tell me he'd made a ten-thousand-dollar donation in my name to some charity that builds schools in Africa for children affected by the diamond economy."

"Oh my God," Steph said, her insides searing. "He's obsessed with that charity. He seems to think if he just funnels them money, that absolves him of every misdeed."

"That seems to be the case. But let's not worry about him."

"But how are we going to get you the money for your space?" she asked as she neared the shop. The sounds of Jack Johnson on the radio greeted her ears. "I have some saved up from my last few gigs."

"First of all, *we* are not going to. *I* will. And second, don't worry about me. I'll come up with something."

"I want to help you, though," Steph said as someone opened the door of the shop.

That someone was Jake. He had a white plastic bag from Island Shine in his hand, and his shades hung on the neck of his gray T-shirt. He locked his gaze on hers, and her stomach pirouetted.

"Mom, I need to go."

CHAPTER
TWENTY-FIVE

"Why are you here?"

He wasted no time. "I need a do-over," he said, stepping closer to the woman he wanted and needed in his life.

"I thought you were leaving?"

"I was heading to the airport, but I couldn't leave without finding you and telling you what an astonishingly horrific job I did at apologizing the other day."

A smirk tugged at the corners of her lips.

"Like, it might have won awards as the worst apology ever," he added.

"It might have," she muttered.

"I've been fielding calls from the *Guinness Book of World Records* requesting it be added to their record book."

The smirk turned into a tiny grin. "It belonged there."

"And I had to try again," he said, drinking her in with his eyes. The sunlight shone on her blonde hair, making it appear golden. The freckles on her nose were an adorable constellation. He wanted to kiss them all. "This time, I want to apologize properly. With gifts. Because I'm pretty sure when you're"—he stopped to tap his chest—"a total ass to the woman you're crazy about, the least you can do is give her a gift to say you're sorry."

She raised her chin, a curious look in her blue eyes. "What have you got?"

"Only the finest," he began as he dipped his hand into the flimsy white bag and produced a coconut air freshener. "For your car back home. Now I know what you're thinking. How could I do something so generous? I picked this not only because it smells awesome, but because I also hope to be spending more time in your car, since I still want to spend more time with you."

She reached for it, taking the coconut cutout without touching his fingers. "OK. So my car will smell nice. That's a start."

"I also got you this," he said, fishing for the next item in the bag. A Ghirardelli chocolate bar. "The kind you like," he said, handing it to her.

She took it, and this time he felt the barest trace of a touch from her fingertips. "I like Ghirardelli."

"I remember . . . and most of all, I want to properly apologize with this card," he said, and grabbed a greeting card of a black-and-white cartoon cat. The inside was blank. But he'd written his own inscription.

When she opened the card, the small grin morphed into a full-blown smile, complete with laughter, as she read aloud the note. "Sorry I behaved like a cat."

She closed the card and looked him in the eyes. A surge of happiness spread through him. He hadn't won her yet, but he hoped he was at least halfway there.

"I'm sorry, Steph. I'm truly sorry. I want to try again with you. For real," he said, then reached for her arms, unable to resist touching her. He ran his fingers along her warm skin. "Because I'm in love with you."

In seconds, her arms were around his neck, and her lips were on his, and all the past was erased in a kiss that marked this starting over.

Tender and warm, it melted his heart.

She broke the kiss and pressed her forehead to his, keeping her arms laced around him, the gifts in her hands. "I'm sorry, too. I'm sorry for all the times I doubted you. And I'm sorry when I acted like a cat as well. But I'm so glad you're here, and I want to try again and not be cats."

He laughed deeply and brushed another kiss on her lips. "Let's do it."

She let go of the embrace and stuffed his gifts into the bag. She dipped her head to his neck and whispered in his ear. "How do you feel about make-up sex?"

⌒◅

"I just need to drop something in the back room of the shop, OK?" she said to Devon as she race-walked through his shop. The afternoon rush was over, so the store was empty.

He was working behind the counter. His eyes drifted from her to Jake. She held Jake's hand.

"Hey, Devon. Nice to meet you. Steph says good things about you," Jake said, and she squeezed his hand.

Devon rolled his eyes. "You think I was born yesterday? Yes, you can use the back room. Just be quiet."

"You're the best," she called out, and in seconds, she'd shut and locked the storage room where Devon kept extra snorkels, masks, and fins.

She backed up against the wall and yanked Jake against her, and all the softness of their reunion kiss vanished in this greedy kiss. It had only been two days without him, but she'd missed him, and she'd longed for this. For this kind of connection, for this kind of moment. Frenzied, desperate, and hungry.

This was the way it should be. Lovers might hurt each other, but they find ways to move on and stay together. She was so glad that all their mistakes were forgivable, because she wanted this—the chance to explore all that they could have together. She'd been wary from the start, reluctant to give her heart. But just because Eli and Duke had been dishonest didn't mean Jake was. He was good, and forthright, and she refused to let the past stop her from trusting the man she loved.

She was going all in.

"I missed you," she said.

"I missed you, too," he murmured as he pushed up the skirt of her sundress and tugged down her bikini bottoms. "Show me. Show me how much," he rasped in her ear, then his fingers were between her legs, and she gasped, and he groaned, and she couldn't wait any longer.

In a mad rush, she unzipped his shorts, and he produced a condom, and then he was sliding into her.

The start of a needy moan tried to escape her lips, but he covered her mouth with his palm as he thrust. "We have to be quiet," he whispered, and she nodded her agreement.

Hell, she'd say yes to anything right now, so long as he didn't stop. He was deep inside her, and pleasure sparked wildly all through her body. She looped her arms around his neck, and he took her like that, against the door, in a snorkel shop, delivering the best make-up sex ever. Soon, she was digging her nails into his back, biting down on his shoulder, and riding to the other side of bliss with him.

Right here with him.

Where she belonged.

$$\infty$$

She was happy.

Radiantly happy.

She might not have accomplished all that she'd come to the Caymans for, but she'd gained something else in return. She'd been solely focused on her business since it blew apart, but she'd learned business was better when she had someone she loved and trusted by her side. Jake was that guy, no questions asked.

After she said good-bye to her old friend, she held hands with Jake as they walked along the boardwalk outside the snorkel shop, under the clear blue sky.

In her other hand, she held the bag of gifts he'd given her. She loved the gifts. Each one was perfect for her.

Then it hit her.

Like an anvil dropped from a ten-story building.

Like a meteor crashing into the yard.

Right under her nose.

She stopped in her tracks.

She whispered his name as a sense of awe descended on her.

"Yes?"

Jake had taught her that knowing the target was the best weapon you had at your disposal. And boy, did she ever know the target. "I know where the diamonds are."

CHAPTER
TWENTY-SIX

"Are you sure you want to?" she asked the question yet another time.

His answer remained the same. "Abso-fucking-lutely."

"We're only going to have a few minutes," she warned.

"Well aware of that."

"And this is our only shot," she added as they rounded up supplies. A quick Google search had taken them to a boutique in Georgetown, then another one near Sapphire, and now they were parking outside a little souvenir shop. Her shoulders tightened with worry that she wouldn't find the Trojan horse.

"Like a lunar eclipse. Only comes around once every few years," he said as he opened the car door for her.

"Exactly. And it could come up empty. I don't even know if I'll find what I need."

"Anything can come up empty," he said, squeezing her hand. "Except this," he said softly, brushing a kiss on her cheek.

She shivered against him.

"Couldn't resist."

"Don't resist."

They popped into the shop, and she made a beeline for the shiny objects. She spun a rack around, hunting. "C'mon, c'mon," she whispered under her breath.

Then she found what she needed to gain entry. "Got it!"

He pumped a fist, and they headed to the counter.

"And you're going to have to be quiet as a deer," she said, reminding him. Like he needed a reminder to be stealthy.

He scoffed. "As if I'd be anything but."

"I'd love to be the gun, but I think I have to be the sniper."

"Babe, you and me. We've got this," he said, squaring his shoulders, confidence seeming to radiate through him. "We do it like our greatest hits. This one-two punch we've got going is the perfect ploy."

"But what if he hears you? Or what if I can't distract them?"

"Then we improvise," he said as they left the store. "That's what we've always done."

"And you're sure you want to do this? You were done with this case and walking away. I don't want to twist your arm into doing something you don't want to do."

"Steph, I promise you this. When it comes to adventure, it's pretty much impossible to twist my arm. I was born to take risks," he said, patting his backpack, then pointing to the fiery orange ball dipping closer to the horizon. "Now let's do it. Sun is setting, and clock is ticking."

C⑨

As Steph walked past the orchids and palm trees, she reflected on the last time she'd been here at Eli's home in this tropical paradise. Two days ago. She'd arrived at her stepfather's, contrite and apologetic. His car and his jewels had been stolen on her watch. Guilt had ravaged her, and doubt had riddled her.

Then, he'd shown his true stripes.

He'd loaned her his car not just because of the better air-conditioning, but to nab the woman who was trying to steal his own stolen gems. He'd told her he'd finally pay the debt he owed her mother, only to send it to a foreign charity. Then, his new lady had let it slip that he'd absconded with the funds in the first place from the company he'd built on the generosity of Steph's mom.

Eli was charming. Eli was delightful. Somewhere, underneath that cad exterior, he had a heart. He wasn't entirely a *bad* guy, but he also traipsed through life with blinders on, oblivious to those he hurt.

This was her last chance to make sure that the bucket of luck in the world didn't tip over for just one guy.

That it ran back in favor of those who'd been screwed. Everyone he took from.

She rang the doorbell and checked the time. In ten minutes, he'd be leaving for the event at Isla's gallery—the one to raise money for their favorite pet charity. If she could have sneaked in when he was gone, she would have. But he had an alarm, and she didn't know the code. The only way to pull this off was to be invited.

A flurry of nerves lodged in Steph's chest, but she ignored them, steadying herself for this last mission.

He opened the door. "Good evening." He beamed, holding it open wide and inviting her inside.

Step one—enter the home.

He dropped a quick kiss on one cheek, then the other.

"You look handsome," Steph said, gesturing to his tailored suit and crisp button-down shirt.

"Why thank you. Wait 'til you see Isla. She's stunning as always."

"I have a gift for her," Steph said, then lowered her voice. "I think you'll be quite happy to see what I got her."

Step two—butter him up.

She showed him the small gift bag with a bow on it. "But wait 'til Isla comes downstairs."

Eli's eyes lit up in excitement. The man simply loved gifts. "Isla, my love," he called out. "Steph is here to say good-bye. And she has a gift for you."

"Be right there," Isla said from upstairs in her cheery voice.

"Are you excited about the fund-raiser?" Steph asked, bouncing on her toes to show she was simply thrilled, too.

"Oh yes. It's going to be wonderful," he said as he waxed on about how much money they hoped to raise, while putting on his cuff links. He got stuck on one, so he removed his Rolex, setting it on the marble table by the door.

"Let me help you," Steph said as she reached for the cuff link and slid it through the button hole in the shirt.

"You're a dear."

A minute later, Isla descended the staircase like a princess at a cotillion. Her black hair was swept high on her head in a twist, with tendrils curled at her cheeks. Her diamond necklace adorned her throat, and a black dress hugged her perfect body.

"Oh Isla," Steph said loudly. So damn loudly as she clasped her hand to her chest. "You look stunning."

∽

The volume was his cue.

The second Steph raised her voice, he climbed into the bathroom window. In seconds, he retraced his steps from the other night. Only this time, it was dusk, and he didn't have the benefit of darkness to cloak him. His heart pounded mercilessly against his chest as he padded across the bathroom floor, down the carpeted hallway, and to Eli's office. Soundlessly, he wrapped a hand around the knob. It didn't budge.

Obstacle one.

He removed his lock-picking kit and worked the door. Once unlocked, the door gently slid open. His breath fled his chest when the door began to squeak. A sliver of a sound.

He cringed but slipped inside and managed to shut the door behind him.

He released a quiet breath and set to work.

Time was not only of the essence. It was the essence.

∽

Everyone has a weakness.

For some, the weakness is food. Like Eli. His penchant for sweets had driven him to make many of his choices.

When it came to Isla, the woman seemed to adore shiny objects.

Steph had learned that the best way to the inside was by knowing the target. The more you know, the greater the chance you can crack a safe, open a door, distract a person. You don't need guns; you don't need weapons. You need to use your head.

"This is just a small thank-you for being so generous with your time, and taking such good care of Eli, and generally for being you," Steph said, laying it on thick as she handed her the gift.

Isla seemed the kind of woman who liked praise. The kind of person for whom flattery truly would get you anywhere.

Step three—give the gift.

Isla batted her lashes and gazed lovingly at the white box with the blue bow. She held it to her chest briefly, like she was hugging it. She didn't even know what it was. "Thank you. It's so sweet of you to do this."

"The pleasure is all mine. But I can't take the credit. A little bird told me you might like them," she said, gesturing to her stepfather.

He raised an eyebrow curiously.

"You two are the best," Isla said as she tugged on the bow.

Steph's pulse soared as she pictured Jake upstairs doing the dirty work. He was right. It had been far easier the last time when she hadn't known what he was up to. This go-around she was nearly sweating nerves.

But she couldn't let them see her sweat.

She narrowed her focus to Isla as the woman daintily unwrapped the bow.

That's right. Take your sweet time.

She dropped the bow on the table. Pulled off the top. And gasped.

Really, it was nothing.

But it was everything.

Isla unwrapped a pair of mermaid earrings similar to the ones Steph had worn.

The Trojan horse.

That was all Steph needed to keep the happy couple occupied at the front door so Jake was free to work his side of the equation upstairs.

∽

One minute and thirty-two seconds this time. He opened the door, fully prepared for a whole lot of nothing. With the way the case had gone so far, he wouldn't be surprised if the safe was empty. But it wasn't empty. He found exactly what he came for, and he wanted to kiss the sky as he filled his backpack, shut the safe, placed the coffee table photograph books in front of it, and rose. In half a minute, he'd be out the window.

A scream rang through the house.

∽

Isla tapped her watch. "We really should go."

Eli nodded. "Yes. We can't be late to our own event."

Isla's nostrils flared. She sniffed the air. She placed her hand on Eli's arms. "Darling. You forgot your aftershave. You never go to an event without it. It's your signature scent. Go put some on."

Steph's eyes widened. Alarms blared in her head as Eli turned on his heels and lickety-split sprinted up the steps. Jake was in the office. Eli was on his way. She had to warn him. She flashed back to his words. *"Then we improvise."*

Quick. She had to think fast. Eli rounded the landing.

Make a noise. Make a sound. Something that would get everyone to freeze. That would lure Eli back down to the first floor and alert Jake.

When it hit her, she had to reign in the wild grin that threatened to burst across her face. Instead, Steph adopted a look of abject fear, pointed to the dining room table, and shouted in her best blood-curdling cry: "Spider!"

Isla shrieked. Eli doubled back. And somewhere upstairs, Steph imagined Jake scrambling. Then, with Isla and Eli hunting for the spider, she made a split-second decision. Her hand shot out to the marble table, like a frog's tongue nabbing a fly.

The woman had some serious lungs on her. Thank Christ for that. He hightailed it out of the office, shut the door, slinked across the hallway, padded through the bathroom, and climbed out the window. He crouched low, out of view of neighbors, and made his way to the other side of the roof, shielded by trees. He lay flat on the roof and waited 'til they left.

Five minutes later, a car pulled out of the garage, and in sixty seconds, he clambered down the tree and slipped into the passenger seat of another vehicle, his getaway driver pulling away.

CHAPTER TWENTY-SEVEN

"Spider?"

"She hates spiders," Steph said matter-of-factly as they drove out of Corey's Landing. "I had to improvise."

"It worked."

"And did it work for you? Did you get them?"

He lifted his backpack and flashed her a grin. "Got 'em all. Left the passport behind, though."

"Are the diamonds *inside* them?" she asked, breathless with excitement. Adrenaline still coursed through her veins and probably would for days.

"Well, I wasn't going to check without my partner."

"Good answer," she said, and they pulled into a parking lot at the nearby beach. Steph cut the engine.

As Jake unzipped his backpack, she told herself she'd be fine with whatever the outcome was. She'd gained so much from this trip and this chance with him that anything more would be icing.

She wanted the icing, though.

She was a big fan of icing.

He dug into the pack and grabbed a handful of chocolate bars procured from the safe in Eli's office. The same kind of bars he'd found the first night. But back then, Steph didn't suspect Eli had hidden his diamonds in his chocolate bars.

But once she'd set eyes on Jake's Ghirardelli chocolate gift, the possibility came to her that he'd squirreled the gems away in his "happy place."

"The real ones are safe and sound and so well hidden that no one will figure it out. Didn't even need to put them in a bank."

Chocolate was the perfect hiding spot for Eli. It suited him to a T—hiding his jewels inside something he loved. Someplace he thought no one would look. And since he'd used nuts as his diamond decoy, she reasoned that he'd tucked the diamonds away in the same tongue-in-cheek, *aren't-I-clever* fashion.

He loved being smarter than everyone else and pulling off his own heists.

Placing the bars on the center console, Jake presented the chocolate with a flourish. "You can do the honors."

A wild ribbon of nerves unspooled inside her. She gulped, steeling herself for whatever she found inside. She unwrapped the first bar from Ecuador and broke it in half. Her heart sank. "Looks like chocolate," she muttered.

"Break it up more," he said, encouraging her. She crumbled the bar into tiny pieces in the wrapper.

"It's still only chocolate," she said, and she wished, she really wished, she could hide the forlorn sound in her voice.

"I know," he said, his tone positive. "But this bar is the same kind I nabbed the first time I tried the safe. We need to test one that says on the wrapper it has nuts." He squeezed her shoulder. "Don't forget what you told me about what you learned from working with me."

"Use what you know about the target," she repeated, searching through the stack of chocolate bars for one with nuts. If she was right, the bar would be nut-free but diamond-full.

She opened the silvery wrapper, her fingers slipping once. She steadied herself, gripped the shiny paper, and ripped it. One long inhale of air, and then like a jackhammer she broke the chocolate bar into pieces.

Diamonds rained down.

Shiny, glittering gems.

Chocolate-covered jewels.

A wild exhilaration flooded her veins in a deluge as she and Jake demolished more chocolate bars. Some were chocolate, but some were full of chocolate and riches. When they finished the stack, they had a pile of diamonds in her car and a pound of chocolate.

"How do we know if these are fake, too?" she asked as a new worry set up camp.

"Don't worry. I know just the guy."

∽

Jake had always loved bras.

Loved them for what they held inside. Loved them because they were the last line of defense protecting some of his favorite things on the planet.

Tonight, he was ready to worship at the throne of the black lace bra Steph donned. It was the perfect home for millions.

"You're such a hot mule," he said, blowing her a kiss.

They'd packed up the loose gems into two small black pouches; then Steph had tucked them into the cups of her bra. "It's the safest place around. So much safer than a . . ." She trailed off and pretended to bang the drums on her punch line. "A safe."

Jake mimed dunking a basketball. "She shoots. She scores." He offered her his elbow. "Shall we go see our diamond man?"

"Let's do it," she said.

They left his hotel room and headed to the downstairs bar. If the diamonds checked out as real, he'd call Andrew and let him know he'd managed to turn a sinking ship around big-time. He scanned the crowd for the man with the thick black hair and beard. He spotted Wilder at the end of the counter, nursing what looked to be an orange juice. Jake walked up to him and shook his hand.

"Thanks for meeting me. Especially at the last minute," Jake said.

"Yes, you very nearly rustled me from my beauty sleep. I have a sharp nine p.m. bedtime," the man said with a wide grin. Wilder shifted his attention to Steph and bowed slightly.

"Pleasure to meet you," he said.

"And you as well."

Jake gestured to a table in the far corner of the establishment. "Why don't we go to where it's a little quieter," he suggested, and they parked themselves away from the noise and hubbub of the bar.

Jake reached into his pocket and removed one loose diamond. The gems in Steph's bra weren't going anywhere. They were cozying up to her breasts to stay out of the way.

Pinching his thumb and forefinger together, Wilder took the jewel. Jake tried to read his expression as the man assessed the diamond, studying it through a small magnifying glass. When Wilder set down the glass, the corners of his lips curved up. "Color is good. Clarity is good. Weight is good. You have a very real, very expensive ten-thousand-dollar diamond from the Frayer mine."

Jake sighed in relief, then grabbed Steph's hand and squeezed it.

"Thank you. A million times over, thank you."

"It is my pleasure. I assume you will buy me another orange juice," Wilder said, holding up his nearly empty glass.

"Consider it done."

While they waited for the drink refill, Jake called Andrew and told him to catch the next flight to the Caymans. He wanted to hand off those puppies as soon as possible. Jake's job was nearly done, and Andrew could ferry them back to the United States of America and begin his task of converting them back to money, then distributing the funds to their rightful owners.

When he ended his call, Wilder was studying a Rolex.

Jake arched an eyebrow. "What's that?"

There was a gleam of triumph in Steph's eyes. "Just a little something my stepdad wanted to give me. I was curious what it's worth."

"Where did you get it?" he asked out of the side of his mouth.

"Someone taught me how to pickpocket," she whispered.

"You took his watch?"

"Well, it was just lying there on the marble table in the entryway. I felt it was calling out to me."

Wilder raised his face. "This watch is quite valuable, too," he said, then gave them a price that nearly made Jake's jaw drop.

"Thank you," Steph said, then deposited the watch in her purse.

Later, as she popped into the restroom near the bar, he pulled Wilder aside. "Did you bring it?"

"I did, indeed. Is this for your sister?" Wilder asked as he reached into his pocket and handed Jake a small pouch. Jake peeked inside, pleased at the contents.

"Nope. This one is not for my sister. But I'm glad we were finally able to do business together."

He shook the man's hand, then said good night.

⌒⊙

Andrew arrived bright and early the next morning. He called as soon as he caught a cab, and told Jake he'd be at the hotel in fifteen minutes.

"Great. Come to room 412, and I will gladly give you all these bad boys," Jake told him, eager to complete the final step in his job—giving the objects to the client who'd hired him to retrieve them.

"Can't wait."

His taxi must have been zippy, because he knocked on the door ten minutes later. When Jake opened the door, Monica greeted him.

CHAPTER
TWENTY-EIGHT

He slammed the door shut.

His heart rate spiked. His blood pounded. Monica was fucking relentless.

"Who is it?" Steph asked as she joined him in the entryway.

He dragged a hand through his hair and blew out a long stream of air. "Monica. The diamond saleswoman. I thought she was done, but she's still hunting them and must know—"

A loud rapping blasted through the room.

"This is Monica Potkin. I'm an investigator with the Securities and Exchange Commission. Please open the door."

Steph's eyes widened. "Shit, is she going to arrest us?" she whispered.

"I don't think they can make arrests, can they?" he said in a low voice, too.

"Don't worry. I'm not here to arrest you," Monica said.

"She has good hearing," Jake said.

"Please open the door so we can talk."

"What do we do?" Steph asked, holding her hands out wide.

"She knows we're here. It's not like we're going to escape through the balcony on the fourth floor at this point," he reasoned.

Steph shrugged. "What else can we do?"

"I know you're not going to climb out the balcony, so it would be awesome if you open the door."

There was no way around this, so Jake reached for the handle, turned it, and opened the door to the woman who might decide his fate. She strode into the room with purpose. Her hair was slicked back. Her demeanor was cool, and she nodded at both of them behind those cat's-eye glasses.

"You've been following me," Jake said, parking his hands on his hips, turning the tables on her. Like he could catch her.

"Right you are. We received a tip that Eli Thompson had stolen money from his hedge fund, turned it to gems with the help of a notorious luxury goods merchant, and skipped the country with diamonds lining his pockets. I've been here in the Caymans working undercover to investigate this case for a few weeks now. When you came into the diamond store with the gem, I knew we were getting closer. But it hasn't been an easy path. Eli Thompson set traps for everyone, and I want to know if he set a trap for you, too."

Jake looked to Steph, and Steph looked to Jake, and they both seemed to know instinctively to keep quiet. Monica might not be the thief, but she possessed powers they didn't have.

"Oh, c'mon," she said, exasperated. "I'm not going to arrest you. I just want to know if you were hired by the Eli Fund to recover the jewels, and if you succeeded."

She knew the Eli Fund had hired its own team? Before he could answer or even decide *what* to answer, there was another rap on the door.

"This better be Andrew," he muttered, and marched to the door, yanked it open, and tugged Andrew into the room. He'd never been more grateful to see a client in his life.

"Andrew, meet Monica Potkin with the SEC," Jake said through tight lips. "She's here for *you*."

"Ah! So glad you're here, too," Andrew said, striding over to Monica and pumping her hand.

"Wait!" Steph interjected. "You know her?"

"We talked on the phone yesterday," Andrew said, then turned to Jake. "When you told me about the theft of the fake rocks, I contacted the SEC and turned the case over to them. They informed me they had an investigator working on it all along and they were already aware and suspicious. So much for my efforts to do this quietly." Andrew's focus shifted to Monica. "If there's any way we can keep this on the down low, I'd be most grateful."

"That's not really a promise I can make, but I'll consider it," she said.

"You know, I'm kind of feeling like my work here is done," Jake chimed in. "What do you say we hand the gems over to you, and the two of us can get on out of town?"

Monica shook her head. "Not so fast. I need a few details. But I meant it when I said you aren't under arrest. Nor are you in trouble. I know you might find this hard to believe, Mr. Harlowe, but we're both on the same side of the law in this case. The right side. Now, tell me more about the diamonds."

⌐⑨

The silvery stingray swam over to Steph. She beamed and brushed a kiss on its slick body. She smiled for the lens as Jake took her picture with a disposable, waterproof camera. He went next, dropping a lip-lock on the creature. Then, they aimed for a hat trick, taking a selfie of a joint stingray smooch.

"I already feel pretty lucky," she said a few hours after they'd left Monica and Andrew to sort out the paperwork.

"Me, too. But just in case, I'd better kiss you."

"You'd better."

They kissed in the shallow blue waters.

Later that afternoon, she put Jake on his flight back to the States, and Steph stayed a few more days to conduct her new tours.

During that time, the investigator held true to her word. Monica had only wanted information, and those details would likely be used to file charges against Eli Thompson. That saddened Steph immensely, knowing what was likely coming next for her stepdad. But he'd made his choice, and she'd fought hard to help him avert such a fate.

In the days that followed, Monica worked with Andrew to convert the diamonds back into cash, and then return the money to the rightful owners.

A most successful recovery of stolen assets, she'd deemed it.

After Steph returned home to Miami, she promptly found a pawn shop to pay her a good price for the Rolex. A small morsel of guilt coursed through her. It was a stolen watch, after all. But then again, Eli *had* offered it, so she didn't feel too bad. In fact, she didn't feel bad at all when she paid the lease on her mom's new jewelry shop.

"You didn't have to do that," her mother said as they settled in for mocktails on South Beach one fine afternoon.

"I didn't have to, but I wanted to. Now, let's watch the people go by."

They made up stories about a *Miami Vice*–style man in a white suit and a pink shirt, then two women in fluorescent-green bikinis riding skateboards, and then a very handsome man wearing cargo shorts, flip-flops, and a T-shirt, who was walking in her direction.

"That man is heading our way to find the love of his life," her mom declared.

The man whipped off his shades, and Steph nudged her mom.

"You get to meet my boyfriend," she said, and then Jake joined them at their favorite spot on South Beach.

Ah, life was good. Life was very, very good.

EPILOGUE

One Month Later

A blue tang fish swept past her, its fins brushing her leg. A parrot fish darted by next.

The water off the coast of Miami was calm today, and the view under the sea was as spectacular as ever. Today's dive was hers. No customers, no video, just Steph and her brother, Robert, exploring one of their favorite spots.

With the regulator in her mouth, she swam past a coral reef and began to make her way skyward.

It was her first "fun" dive in weeks, but she couldn't complain about the work ones, either. Business had been good and had steadily picked up—both here in Miami and around the Caribbean. She'd been fortunate enough to book a few tours in Turks and Caicos and the Bahamas, and those had kept her busy. They'd also kept her away from Jake, but she knew the score. She knew what she'd signed up for, and she loved every second of their moments together. They were apart more than not, but they made the most of the days when the stars aligned to bring them back to Florida. He'd been gone for the last week, tracking a missing Rembrandt in Switzerland, and she hoped to see him in a few days.

She'd landed a Caymans tour next month, and she didn't think she'd see Eli there. His string of luck had mostly run out. He'd been sentenced to securities fraud, but he'd lawyered up once more and had landed a lighter penalty. He had to spend one year in jail, and then he and Isla would serve out the rest of his sentence with extended community service. They were being sent to Africa to build schools for the charity they'd funded.

That had seemed fitting when Steph read the news.

Steph reached the surface with Robert a few feet behind her. They swam to Lance's boat twenty feet away as the afternoon sun cast golden rays across the water. They chatted about the new woman Robert was seeing, and when they reached the hull, Steph grasped the hand that Lance offered her.

But when she turned her face, she saw Jake was the one hoisting her back onto the boat.

"You're back! I didn't think you'd be back for a few more days."

"I didn't think I'd return this soon, either," he said as she climbed over the edge and joined him on the deck. Robert followed behind.

"Did you find the Rembrandt?"

"Under a floorboard in an old villa in Tuscany."

"Did you use your hammer?" she asked as she shed her dive gear.

He nodded. "I sure did."

"Hey, Harlowe!"

The shout came from Robert, who was dripping wet on the deck of the boat now, too.

"Yeah?"

"This is the part where you kiss the girl."

Jake saluted Steph's brother. "Then I'd better take her to my boat," he said, and she spotted a smaller boat, moored next to Lance's, attached by a rope.

"You bought a boat?" Steph asked, because that didn't seem his style. She grabbed her bag with her sundress, sunscreen, and phone in it.

"Nah, just rented it for the afternoon because I couldn't wait to see you."

"How did you know I was here at this spot, though?"

His lips quirked up. "Called Robert yesterday. He told me. I wanted to surprise you."

"All right, you two need to get off my boat before you start making out," Lance said in a surly growl.

"We're leaving, we're leaving," she said, climbing up on the starboard side and stepping onto Jake's boat. He joined her, and Lance helped untie the two vessels.

Lance cranked the motor and took off with her brother, waving good-bye.

She was alone with the man she loved, on the ocean, under the sun, bobbing in the gentle waves. "So, is this my surprise? You? Because I like that kind of surprise," she said, lacing her arms around his neck and planting an *it's-so-good-to-see-you-again* kiss on his lips.

"Mmm," he murmured as he showed her how much he'd missed her, too.

But then he broke the kiss and dug into his pocket. "I had this made for you," he said, handing her a small black velvet bag. "By your mom."

Excitement pinged through her. She didn't know what was in the bag, but the fact that he'd gone to her mom meant the world to her.

"Open it."

She tugged on the drawstring, dipped two fingers inside, and pulled out a silver necklace with a small charm. She gasped as the sun reflected off a new treasure chest necklace. "I love it."

"Look inside," he told her, and this necklace was different from the one she'd lost. This one had a treasure chest that opened, and the top dangled from the end of the chain. She popped the top.

A brilliant red gem sparkled, lit up from the sun.

A ruby.

"My birthstone," she said, flashing back to their conversation at the beach in the Caymans.

"Told ya I knew birthstones," he said, rocking back on his heels, a note of pride in his tone. He stepped closer and threaded his hand through her wet hair. "And I know you," he whispered. "I got it our last night in the Caymans. Bought it from Wilder at the bar."

"You did? You've been planning this for a whole month?"

He nodded, smiling broadly as he tapped the charm. "Read the inscription on the bottom."

She flipped it over and covered her mouth with her palm. A tear slid down her cheek. A tear of happiness. "You're my treasure," she whispered as her throat hitched. "I love it."

"Let me put it on you," he said, and she lifted her hair. He unhooked the necklace, then clasped it around her neck, letting it fall to her chest. He ran his fingers along the charm. "Beautiful. Like you. Now, what do you say we sail off into the sunset and spend the evening on the boat on the ocean?"

"Will you do bad things to me?"

"Don't I always?"

"You do, but even when it's bad it's good."

"And it always will be," he said as he parked himself in the driver's seat and held her hand as she sat next to him.

He started up the motor, then met her eyes. "By the way, funny thing about rubies," he said as they began cutting through the water.

"What's the funny thing about rubies, Jake?"

"Got a tip that a guy in Spain had some rubies stolen from him. I'm talking to him about getting them back."

She arched an eyebrow. "I take it that means you'll be in Spain for a while?"

"I might be. It might also be more fun if I had a partner with me."

He squeezed her hand as they rode over the ocean, chasing the sun to the horizon. She weighed the possibility of traveling to Spain with him. "Does that mean you want me to be your partner in this ruby affair?"

"Ruby affair. I like the sound of that."

ACKNOWLEDGMENTS

I have always loved heist movies. They are among my favorites, and I've looked for the chance to pull off a heist tale, showing characters using their wits and brains while on a wild caper. To that end, I am thankful for the films that have inspired me over the years, such as *Ocean's Eleven*, *The Thomas Crown Affair*, *How to Steal a Million*, *The Italian Job*, and many others.

The Sapphire Affair grew out of a simple conversation with Helen as we tossed about ideas for such a caper. "I'd like to write about a jewel thief," I said, and many twists and turns on the path to publication later, that idea took shape into Jake and Steph's story.

Thank you to Helen, Irene, and Alison for shepherding this concept through all of its phases and cheering it on. Thank you to Michelle Wolfson for darting and weaving and making things happen as only you can do. Thank you to Jessica, Anh, and the entire team at Montlake for championing *The Sapphire Affair* and sharing your excitement every step of the way.

I am indebted to my editors. Thank you, Alison, for your passion and enthusiasm, as well as your professionalism! It's easy to work with you! I am grateful for my talented story editor, Selina McLemore, who knew precisely what the books needed to shine. Thank you, Selina, for being tough, as I want you to be! You're also brilliant!

Much gratitude to K. P. Simmon at Inkslinger for reading early pages and for helping me, as always, figure out what to do with all these books! Abiding thanks to Bella Andre for the spot-on advice given at RWA. Thank you to the fabulous foursome for all the support and encouragement—I would not be able to navigate this world without K. Bromberg, Laurelin Paige, and C. D. Reiss. Huge hugs and love to Monica Murphy, Lili Valente, Sawyer Bennett, Kendall Ryan, Violet Duke, Lexi Ryan, Tawna Fenske, and the inimitable Marie Force!

Most of all, thank you to my family, especially my husband, who put up with daily—wait, hourly—conversations that often started with, "What if Jake went here . . . ?" Or, "And then what should happen next to Steph . . . ?"

And, as always, thanks to my dogs!

ABOUT THE AUTHOR

Lauren Blakely writes sexy contemporary romance novels with heat, heart, and humor. She is the author of eight *New York Times* bestsellers and sixteen *USA Today* bestsellers. Her series include Sinful Nights, Seductive Nights, No Regrets, Caught Up in Love, and Fighting Fire, as well as stand-alone romances like *21 Stolen Kisses* and *Big Rock*. She also writes for young adults under the name Daisy Whitney. Lauren believes life should be filled with family, laughter, and the kind of love that romantic songs promise. She lives in California with her husband, children, and dogs.